"Another one? eyes flashed fire

Just as she thought everything was going well, now there was something else.

"And is this Monique jealous? Is *she* besotted with you, too?" Sara glared at him. "I mean, how many more women do you need protection from? Perhaps I should be on bonus or danger money or something—"

Morgan gave a deep sigh and put his hands on her arms. "Hold still, little wildcat! I'm not sure how to begin to tell you—"

"Answer me! Is she another one of your women?" Sara wrenched herself free. "Whatever do you need *me* for? Why not call one of your harem?"

Sara wished she had never agreed to pose as his fiancée—in fact, she wished she'd never even met the infuriating Morgan Haldane!

Books by Mary Wibberley

HARLEQUIN ROMANCES

HARLEQUIN PRESENTS

These books may be available at your local bookseller.

For a free catalog listing all titles currently available, send your name and address to:

Harlequin Reader Service
P.O. Box 52040, Phoenix, AZ 85072-2040
Canadian address: P.O. Box 2800, Postal Station A,
5170 Yonge St., Willowdale, Ont. M2N 5T5

Man of Power

Mary Wibberley

Harlequin Books

TORONTO • NEW YORK • LONDON
AMSTERDAM • PARIS • SYDNEY • HAMBURG
STOCKHOLM • ATHENS • TOKYO • MILAN

Original hardcover edition published in 1980
by Mills & Boon Limited

ISBN 0-373-02388-X

Harlequin Romance first edition February 1981
Second printing August 1982
Third printing December 1982
Fourth printing February 1984

CHAPTER ONE

'SARA, what on earth are you doing up there?' Aunt Rachel had a carrying voice, doubtless due to the many speeches she made. Sara didn't answer; she was too sick at heart to care whether her aunt thought her rude or not. She heard the heavy footsteps on the stairs and mentally braced herself, then her aunt walked in. 'You *are* here! You must have heard me calling you. Why didn't you answer?' She stood there, large and formidable, her bosom heaving with the unaccustomed effort of climbing the steep stairs to the attic, and her knuckles were white on the ebony-topped cane she invariably used.

Sara turned slowly. 'I was thinking.'

Two spots of colour burned in Aunt Rachel's cheeks. 'You're a dreamer—just like your father always was. You know I have guests coming in an hour. Shake yourself, girl, you know I can't get everything ready myself.'

'Then why don't you get them to help?' enquired Sara.

'*Them?* Whom precisely do you mean by *them*?'

'My cousins.'

'Jeanette is practising her piano, and Elizabeth is going riding in half an hour. Do be reasonable!'

'But they never do help, do they? It's always me——'

'Always?' demanded her aunt. 'What on earth do you mean? You've only been here two weeks——'

'Yes, I know.'

'And we've given you a home. I consider you're very ungrateful——'

'You gave me a home,' replied Sara steadily, 'because my father died and left me penniless—and because you really didn't have much choice, did you? Do you think I wanted

5

to come here? I'd rather have moved into the Y.W.C.A., but that wouldn't have done much for your image as the local Lady Bountiful, would it? Mrs Bourne, wife of the mayor-to-be of Little Mendover, and chairman of most of the charity committees for miles around, letting the orphaned daughter of her penniless artist brother-in-law go to the Y.W.C.A.——' She paused for breath, blinking back tears. This had been boiling up for the past ten days, ever since she had realised exactly why her snobbish aunt had taken her in—when she had read the subtle and cleverly worded article in the local paper. 'I'm not stupid, Aunt Rachel. Please don't treat me like a child, I'm nearly twenty.'

'And damned impertinent! I have *never* heard such——'

'Perhaps because you've never listened to anyone before——'

'*Silence!* How *dare* you speak to me like that! Wait until your uncle gets home!'

Sara stared at her aunt, the unhappiness spilling over in the burning tears she could no longer contain. 'Uncle Herbert is as frightened of you as——' she began.

'I will not hear another word.' Aunt Rachel was white with temper. 'You've said enough. Come down *at once*, you ungrateful little bitch, and——'

'I'm leaving.' Sara went over to the wardrobe and lifted down the battered leather case that was, ironically, her one legacy from her father. 'You can tell your friends what you like—I don't care. I shall go to the Y.W.C.A. tonight, and tomorrow I'll start looking for a job. Then I'll be independent.'

'You're not going anywhere, miss.' Her aunt's face was twisted with the vicious temper she could no longer control. 'You can stay in your room until you learn how to apologise for the wicked things you've just said. And when I let you out you'll have learned exactly what your place is in *this* household. You're nothing to me—never have been

—and how you *dare* speak so disparagingly of your cousins I'll never know. They welcomed you here as though you were their sister!'

'They've treated me like dirt, and you know it,' retorted Sara. 'And if you try to lock me in, I'll break the door down.' She moved towards her aunt, who, moving swiftly for all her bulk, turned, slammed the door shut, and locked it. From the other side her voice came, distorted and shaking with her overwhelming temper:

'Let's see you break *that* down, miss—and you'll regret it!' Then there was the heavy sound of her footsteps moving down the passage, then the stairs. Another door slammed angrily in the distance, and all was silent.

Sara went over to the window and pressed her forehead against the cool glass. She closed her eyes. She was shaking. 'Dad, oh, Dad,' she whispered. 'You wouldn't have wanted me here, I know. What am I to do?' There was no one to answer. She was alone, more alone at that moment than she had ever been in her life. But she wasn't beaten. Her aunt was used to controlling people wherever she went, either by the power of her position as local councillor-cum-wealthy builder's wife, or by use of her clever, acid-sharp tongue. Even her two daughters, obnoxious though they were, were no match for their mother, not yet anyway. Jeanette, at thirteen, wilful and spoilt, was learning fast, and already had traces of her mother's mannerisms, and Elizabeth, one year older than Sara and plain as the proverbial pikestaff, was already the most appalling snob whose one aim in life, it appeared, was to put Sara down every time she spoke. Sara gave a wry smile at that last thought. Elizabeth had tried it once too often just an hour previously, when she and Sara had been alone in the house.

Sara had been in the kitchen making herself a much needed cup of coffee after a marathon bout of Hoovering, when Elizabeth had strolled in, flung her Gucci handbag on a chair, sat down and said:

'You can make me a cup while you're there.'

'Certainly,' Sara answered. 'If you say please.' There was a pained silence lasting several seconds during which Sara calmly added milk to her cup and picked up the morning's paper.

'Oh *dear*,' remarked Elizabeth at last. 'Lessons in manners—from *you*?' She had sat there, face mocking, eyes travelling scornfully up and down Sara's shabby jeans and faded sweater. 'I'm sure I need *those*!'

'Yes, you do,' retorted Sara, and sat down at the table with the paper in front of her. 'But it's a bit late now.'

'Damn you!' snapped Elizabeth, her voice shrill, and snatched the paper from Sara. 'Make me a cup of coffee and be quick about it. I'm going out riding soon, with my *friends*. They'll be awfully amused when I tell them how uppity you're getting since you came here——My God! It doesn't take some people long to acquire airs and graces, does it?' Her pale blue eyes had gleamed spitefully, and the flush on her cheeks only served to make her look plainer than ever. Sara had laughed—which had the same unfortunate effect as adding water to a pan of hot fat. Elizabeth, incensed, had reached out and struck her, and Sara retaliated swiftly by flinging the cup of hot coffee over her cousin. Then she had stood up, looking down at the gasping, spluttering girl with a feeling of satisfaction mingled with pity. The satisfaction was for having done something she should have done days before—the pity was for her pathetic cousin who was too stupid to see that her so-called 'friends' only kowtowed to her for one reason—her father's money.

'Do tell me how amusing your friends find *that*!' said Sara, raising her voice above Elizabeth's wailing as she looked at the coffee soaking into her exquisite silk blouse. 'I'm going up to my room.' She had walked out and up the stairs, and there she had remained until her aunt had come up. Presumably Elizabeth had not told her mother what had happened, or it would surely have been mentioned.

Perhaps, thought Sara shrewdly, it was because she hadn't yet thought of a version in which Elizabeth would emerge in a shining light.

It was time to move. Sara changed into a simple blue cotton dress, packed her clothes neatly in the case and fastened the straps. Then she looked in her purse. There were ten pound notes in it—all she possessed. It was enough for the moment. She went to the door, carrying a sheet of lining paper from her dressing table drawer, and her pen. Kneeling down, she slid the paper under the gap at the bottom of the door, pushed the pen slowly and gently into the keyhole until there was a 'clink', then carefully eased the paper back in. The key was on it. Sara smiled a little smile, mentally thanking the author of the detective book she'd read which had told her the trick, and unlocked the door.

She was almost at the top of the attic stairs when she heard the front doorbell ring. She put the case down and prepared to wait until after this early arrival was ushered in and settled. It would make her exit far easier. Her aunt would definitely not want a fuss with any of her bridge-playing cronies in the house.

Then she heard the man's voice, and went very still. The deep attractive tones carried quite clearly up the two flights of stairs.

'Mrs Bourne? How do you do. My name is Morgan Haldane. I believe you have a Miss Sara Bourne staying here with you?'

'Why, yes—but I'm afraid I don't know you, Mr Haldane——' her aunt's voice was positively arch—and stunned; a difficult combination. Sara frowned. The arch woman made quite a change from the shrill-tongued virago of minutes previously. Either the unseen Mr Haldane had arrived in a Rolls-Royce or he was good-looking. More important, though, was the fact that he was asking for *her*. She had never heard of him. She sat on the top stair, the better to listen, and prepared to creep down when they moved away.

'I have a letter here that will explain it all. My father and Miss Bourne's father were close friends during the war—I only received the news of his death yesterday, and I've flown up from the South of France.'

'You've flown here? To see *Sara*?' Aunt Rachel's voice had taken on a sharper, more wary note. Clearly this was something beyond her comprehension, that anyone would consider her niece important enough to fly to see.

'Yes. May I do so?'

'She's not well, I'm afraid, Mr—er—Haldane. Perhaps you could give me the message. I'm expecting friends at any moment——'

'Is she here?' He didn't exactly interrupt. It was hard to say precisely how he silenced her aunt, but he did it.

'Well, she's had to—I'm afraid she can't——'

'Oh! I'm awfully sorry—I didn't——' Elizabeth's voice came floating up, prettily confused. I'll bet she's fluttering her sandy eyelashes at him, thought Sara. He must be good-looking. She doesn't put on *that* voice for any old rubbish.

'Is this Miss Bourne?' his voice asked.

'Yes—but not Sara. This is my daughter Elizabeth.'

'How do you do, Miss Bourne.'

'How do you do. Did I hear you say—er—you've not come to see *Sara*, have you?' There was that same inflection as her mother's, the touch of shrillness, the surprise—and a certain cooling.

'Why, yes, I have.' He sounded—not amused, exactly; Sara couldn't decide what it was. She was going downstairs to find out for herself in a moment, when the little pantomime was over, because she was intrigued.

'Why do you want to see her?' Sara could picture Elizabeth's face as she said it.

There was a moment's silence. 'Why, Miss Bourne? I've already told your mother that I've flown up from Nice today. I feel that the explanations for my visit will be easier with Miss Sara Bourne present—to save repetition, you understand. Of course, as you are expecting guests I wouldn't dream of intruding—perhaps I might have a brief word with her now, and arrange to see her tomorrow.'

'She's locked in her room. She threw a cup of coffee over me, the little b——'

'*Elizabeth!* Please be quiet! Whatever will Mr—er—Haldane think?'

'Oh, Mother, why pretend she's ill, for God's sake! Let him see her and have done with it. She's just a——'

'Locked? Did you say *locked* in her room?' The effective silencing again. The deep voice definitely not amused.

'It was all a misunderstanding—you'd better come into the dining room. Elizabeth, hadn't you better go now? Daddy will be in soon.'

'I'm in no hurry.' The insolence was there again.

The voices faded, a door closed, and Sara ran swiftly and silently down the stairs to the dining room. Her aunt was speaking.

'—a very awkward girl I'm afraid, Mr Haldane. Now, please tell me your business, exactly, and we'll take it from there.'

'I prefer to tell Miss Bourne herself. In fact I must insist on seeing her as soon as possible.'

'Insist, Mr Haldane? May I remind you that you are in *my* house?'

'Indeed yes, Mrs Bourne, I am well aware of that. And if you request me to leave I will, of course, do so. And I shall probably sit in my car at the front until she comes out.'

Good for you, thought Sara. He actually sounded as if he were not afraid of her aunt—which made him something of a rarity. Sara had visions of her aunt's friends having to park their cars down the drive and walk past a car with this strange man sitting inside. She stifled a laugh. She hadn't laughed for ages, and it was a pity to have to quell it, but she didn't want to give the game away yet.

'I don't like your tone.' Aunt Rachel's voice dripped acid. She recovered fast.

'Nor I yours, Mrs Bourne,' he replied quietly in tones of such grave courtesy that the sting in the words was delayed.

'I shall ask you to leave.'

'Now? Or after I've seen her?'

'Now. At once.'

'May I get this perfectly clear before I go? You have locked Miss Bourne in her room, and you refuse to let me talk to her?'

'Precisely. I have never met such an ill-mannered man as——'

'Then I shall go straight to the nearest police station and tell them that you are holding your niece prisoner, that you will not allow anyone to see her. I shall then tell them who I am and why I'm here, and I will see what they advise. No doubt I shall be returning very shortly with a police officer. It may distress your friends, of course, but——'

It was enough. Sara was too curious to see this man who dared to speak to her aunt thus, without even having raised his voice once, to remain outside the door any longer. She opened it and went in.

'I'll save you the trouble of all that,' she said. 'I'm Sara Bourne, and I'm not locked in my room any more.' She held up the key, then threw it on to the table, where it bounced on the exquisite mahogany top before tinkling gently to a standstill. Then she looked at the man standing there, and she too was silenced. At least she knew one thing, in that first startled moment of seeing him. She knew why both aunt and cousin had fluttered so at first....

He was big. Oh, he was big. She knew too why he wasn't remotely frightened of her aunt. He didn't look frightened of anybody. He looked tough and tall and solid—not a spare ounce of fat on him, all muscle, well evidenced by the tight black sweater and equally tight black jeans he wore.

But his face was even more compelling—tanned hawklike features, high cheekbones, dark, dark eyes, thick eyebrows and equally thick straight hair, raven black, that grew in a widow's peak from his forehead. His mouth appeared to be twitching, whether with anger or suppressed laughter it was impossible to say.

He took the necessary steps forward and they shook hands. Sara brushed the tangle of deep chestnut hair from her forehead. 'I've been listening at the door,' she told him. 'I was just about to leave when you arrived.'

'Leave?' Her aunt's voice cut in, shrill with shock and temper. 'What do you mean—leave?'

'I already told you, Aunt Rachel,' answered Sara calmly, turning to face her. 'I'm going to live at the Y.W.C.A.' The words dropped like stones into a frightening silence that was broken by the man.

'No, Miss Bourne,' he said, 'I don't think so.'

'Why not?' She turned to look him squarely in the eye. 'Would *you* stay on here if you were me?'

'Heaven forbid!' He began to laugh, and Elizabeth, silent for too long, and seething, her pale face blotchy with temper, strode forward and slapped his face.

'How dare you insult us!' she shrilled.

He looked down at her as if a fly had brushed his cheek. 'I haven't even begun to insult you, Miss Bourne, though I would have no difficulty in doing so. And your protestations about my 'insults' would be more convincing if you weren't in such an obviously hysterical state.' He turned to Elizabeth's mother, who held her cane as if she would like to strike him with it. 'And you, madam, will be pleased to know we're leaving right now. Is your case ready, Miss Bourne?'

'It's upstairs. I left it there when I ran down. I'll go and get it——'

'Show me. I'll carry it down for——'

'You're not going anywhere in my house!'

'I am going to fetch your niece's case Mrs Bourne, and bring it down for her. I hardly think you're in a position to stop me. Lead the way,' this to Sara, who turned and went out.

She led him up the lushly carpeted stairs to the first landing, then looked at him. 'Up one more flight,' she said.

'In the attics? That figures. Lead on.'

When they reached the top he picked up the case and Sara picked up her handbag. 'Is this all?' he asked.

'It is.'

'We'll talk outside,' he said.

'Yes. Thank you. If you'd come half an hour later I'd have been gone.'

'Then it's as well I arrived when I did. Are they really as nauseating as they appear?'

'More so, actually. I don't know who you are or why you've come, but I'd appreciate a lift to the——'

'Y.W.C.A.? No, not there.'

'Where then?' she asked, well aware of shrill voices rising from the hall, and the puzzled replies of a man—her uncle had come home and was getting the full blast. She felt terribly sorry for him.

'Do you trust me?' asked Morgan Haldane.

'Oh, I trust you,' she said. 'I'd trust anybody who could speak to my aunt the way you did and get away with it.'

'She's a bully, and bullies are weak. They only pick on those even weaker than themselves—but I don't think you are.'

'She doesn't frighten me, nor do her two daughters,' Sara assured him.

'God! Is there *another* one?'

'Jeanette's thirteen. Not as bad—yet. But my position is an awkward one. I have nothing, and they're my only relatives. They've given me a home.'

'Not any more. You need never come back here.'

'I don't intend to,' she told him. 'We'd better go down.

My uncle's arrived. He's not bad—I like him very much—
please don't——'

'Don't hit him? You mean *he* might take a swing at me
too?'

'They'll have told him some awful story. I can
imagine——'

'Let's go down and find out. Don't worry, he's safe.
Anyone married to that dragon has all the problems he
needs.'

The war party was waiting in the hall, blocking their
exit, Uncle Herbert flanked by his two womenfolk, clearly
a worried and disturbed man. He paled slightly at the sight
of Morgan Haldane, and Sara said:

'Whatever they've told you, Uncle, I think you'd better
listen to me before you say anything. Mr Haldane is the son
of a friend of Dad's.'

'Haldane?' Herbert Bourne seized on the name. '*Haldane*? Son of *Red* Haldane?'

'Yes, sir, I am,' Morgan replied.

Her uncle's face changed, became visibly relaxed, as if
some terrible tension had flowed away from him, and he
held out his hand, and Morgan shook it.

Aunt Rachel gasped. 'Herbert! *What* are you——'

'Be quiet, Rachel.' He turned on his wife—and everyone
else gasped. 'Come into the lounge, Mr Haldane.'

'I'm expecting company any moment!' Aunt Rachel
snapped. Her face had gone the colour of putty, save where
two spots of colour and fury burned on her cheeks.

'Then you may take them in the dining room, my dear.
Come, Sara, Mr Haldane——' and he turned and began to
lead the way towards the lounge. Aunt Rachel moved forward heavily and stood in front of her husband.

'I forbid you——' she began. She was shaking with a
terrible rage. Herbert Bourne drew himself up to his full
height and met his wife's venomous glance calmly. Sara
watched, dazed, scarcely daring to believe her eyes. This,

now, was a totally different man from the one she had seen constantly ridiculed in his own house by his wife and two daughters. The mention of a name had wrought some kind of miracle.

'If you don't move aside immediately, Rachel, I shall hit you,' he said. 'Something I should have done many years ago. And by God, you'll know you've been hit!'

Mrs Bourne's face crumpled. She seemed to shrink before them. 'Herbert——' she began. She was a very perturbed woman.

'Step aside! And if I have *one more word* from either you or Elizabeth, I shall open the door when your precious friends arrive and tell them exactly where they can go— and I shan't mince my words, be sure of that.'

'You're going to be mayor next month——' Aunt Rachel was making a game effort. 'You can't——' her mouth puckered, as if she were about to cry.

'Can't I? Watch me! You are the social climber, my dear, not me. I'm weary of it all. I'm weary of you, and this house, and the ghastly hangers-on you've acquired over the years—and it's taken me all this time to realise it.' He pushed his trembling wife to one side. 'Mr Haldane is the son of one of the finest men who ever lived, and I shall entertain him in *my* house, when *I* choose. And now you and Elizabeth can go and make us three cups of coffee, and you can bring them in here and then leave us. Do you understand me, Rachel?'

When she didn't reply he repeated the question sharply. 'I said, do you understand me?'

'Yes, Herbert.' Her face might have turned to stone. Her lips barely moved.

He led them in. 'Sit down, please.' He then turned to Sara, and Morgan. 'Thank you for coming here, Mr Haldane,' he said. 'You've done me more of a good turn than you can ever imagine.'

Sara went and hugged her uncle impulsively.

'You were marvellous!'

He smiled at her gently. 'I didn't do so badly, did I?' He looked at the silent man who watched them. 'I think I know why you're here. And I thank God you came when you did.'

CHAPTER TWO

SARA had read the letter in a daze, and she still held it when the two subdued women came in carrying a tray of coffee, and then departed—without a word being said.

She looked up at last. 'I can't believe—this is like a dream, Mr Haldane——'

'Morgan. Please call me Morgan,' he said. 'I know it's a surprise. Take your time, read the letter again if you must —I think it says it all. I only received it yesterday. It had been shuttled back and forth between various solicitors while they decided whether or not I, as my father's heir, should have it.'

'But there's no obligation on you,' Sara said quietly. 'And while I'm grateful that you've taken all this trouble to come here, I don't see——'

'It's a debt of honour, Miss Bourne.' He stood very tall, very straight and strong by the fireplace, and there was a great dignity in his words that moved both Sara and her uncle.

'I understand what Morgan means,' he said. 'I knew most of the story years ago, which is why I reacted so strongly upon hearing your name—and possibly why I also reacted so strongly to my wife's words.' He smiled at Sara. 'Sometimes, in life, there are moments when you get a flash of insight that puts everything into perspective, and I had one in the hall when I heard Sara say your name. I've wasted many years trying to cope with the demands of an ambitious and selfish woman—now it's all over. She—and my daughters—toe the line from now on.'

'Phew!' Sara laughed. She still held the letter. 'Perhaps we can't thank you enough, Morgan, but I'm young, and

I'm independent, and I'll cope too.' She smoothed the paper with a gentle finger. It was a letter that had been written by her father, unknown to her; a brief eloquent letter to his companion in the war, Red Haldane, recalling a promise made, a vow given after Philip Bourne had saved Red's life during a violent, bloody encounter with Germans when both men had been working with the French Resistance in Paris.

She had known nothing of all this, but her uncle had sketched in the details when they had first come into the lounge and before she read the letter. Philip and Red Haldane had lost touch after the two had been through so much together—Philip invalided out, and too proud to contact his old comrade in arms—Red to go on to greater glory, saving a group of children from the clutches of the Gestapo in a daring pre-dawn snatch that had left a building full of vital German files razed to the ground and several top Nazi leaders killed along with it. After the war Red had vanished from public life, the shy hero who wanted no more publicity. There had been a brief mention of him in some newspaper two or three years previously, in connection with a hotel in the South of France.

'My father tried to trace your father,' said Morgan, interrupting Sara's thoughts. 'He tried for a long time.'

'We lived very quietly, about fifty miles from here,' Sara answered. 'But Dad had deliberately cut himself off from his old world—Uncle Herbert will tell you—and when my mother died six years ago he became a virtual recluse, but he still painted his beautiful pictures. They were his reason for living.'

Morgan produced a piece of paper from his pocket, sealed in transparent plastic, and handed it to Sara. 'He did this of my father. I brought it to show you—in case you needed any final proof of my identity.' She looked at it, and instantly saw the delicate touch of her father's pen. It was a pen-and-ink sketch of a young dark-haired man, so like his son, but more hawklike, more——

'He was half American Indian,' said Morgan softly. 'My maternal grandmother was a full-blooded Cherokee——' he smiled. 'That's why he was so good at Resistance work. He moved silently and swiftly—and he was deadly with a knife.'

She looked again at the sketch and shivered. I'm glad he was on our side, she thought. And this man, his son, Morgan—no wonder Aunt Rachel hadn't been able to intimidate him.

'And I have come here to offer you a home,' he said, and she felt a tremor of shock run through her. The words she had somehow sensed before, many minutes ago, had finally been said. She looked up. There was a great stillness in the room, a silence following his words, and there was something—a tension, subtly filling the air that made her catch her breath in her throat; and she looked at his face. It was dark, intent, serious. He was—or could be—a frightening man, and for a moment she herself was afraid.

She found her voice at last. 'It's very kind of you,' she answered softly. 'But as I said, there's no need——'

'Sara, I live in a house outside Cannes. It's always full of people—as well as my staff. I'm a busy man. Would you not come for a brief time, say a month, as a holiday—and if you wish to stay after that, I can offer you a job you would find quite attractive, I promise you.' He smiled slightly.

Sara was very still. Her intention was to find a job; she had made that clear to him. What she hadn't said was that this was an area of high unemployment. Even her uncle had had to cut down on staff recently, and she wouldn't have imposed on him. It was almost as if he knew....

Her uncle's words crystallised her thoughts. 'What an opportunity!' he said with a wry smile. 'Elizabeth, would go green with envy,' he laughed.

Yes, she would, but that wasn't what made Sara answer in the way she did. 'Thank you,' she said quietly. 'I accept.'

'Good.' Morgan looked at his watch. 'Have you a current passport?'

'Yes.'

'We'll stay at Heathrow tonight. I hired a car when I arrived. And in the morning we'll fly to Nice.' He spoke as if it were all cut and dried.

Sara laughed. 'That sounds decisive enough. Only one snag—you've not seen my clothes!'

'Hrm!' her uncle's cough stopped her. He produced his wallet and opened it.

'No!' she protested. 'I can't let you—I'll manage——'

'I insist, my dear,' he said, a gleam in his blue eyes so reminiscent of her father that she caught her breath. 'It's the very least I can do for my favourite niece,' and he counted out five twenty-pound notes. 'That should see you started anyway.' He stood up, came over to her, hugged her and forced them into her hand. 'It's never too late to make amends—and you must have had a hellish fortnight here.' He chuckled. 'Don't worry, I'll cut down my two daughters' clothing allowances for a month or so to make up. That'll make them appreciate where their money comes from!'

Sara hugged him back, tears filling her eyes. 'Thank you,' she whispered.

He turned to Morgan. 'We'd be very pleased for you to stay here tonight,' he said.

'Thank you, but I'd prefer to get back as soon as possible. There's a plane in the morning I'd like to be on.' He walked forward and offered his hand to Herbert Bourne. 'It's been a pleasure to meet you, sir,' he said as they shook hands. 'Here's my card with my address. Sara can phone you as often as she wishes.'

Herbert Bourne looked at the card, then he looked up at the man who towered over him. 'Good grief!' he murmured. 'I had no idea——'

Sara would have liked to read what was on the card. What on earth could it say to have caused that respectful pause, the change of tone? Her uncle hugged her and kissed her cheek. 'Enjoy yourself, love,' he said. 'And don't worry about me. I've a few more tricks up my sleeve where it comes to getting this house organised now as I want it.'

'I'm sure you have. Let me know.' She kissed him in return. 'I'll phone, Uncle, just as soon as I'm there.' She turned to Morgan. 'I'm ready to leave now,' she said.

'Right,' he answered. 'Let's go.'

But they didn't stay at Heathrow that night; they flew to Paris instead. Sara, bemused, watched the coast of England recede and tried to sort out her confusion of thought. How had it happened—what had been the first words that had triggered it off? Then she remembered.

As they drove away from Little Mendover in the smart Audi he had hired, Morgan said: 'Watch out for a telephone kiosk, will you? I want to make a phone call.'

'There's one about three miles further on, just before we get to another village. I'll tell you when we reach it.'

'Thanks.' He hadn't looked at her as he spoke. He kept his eyes on the road, hands confident on the wheel, driving swiftly but not too much so. Sara felt safe with him.

'Is it to book rooms at the hotel?' she asked.

'No. How do you feel about flying to Paris tonight?' It was said quite casually, but she gasped.

'What? *Paris!* I thought you said——'

'I know, but I changed my mind. I'm going to phone ahead and see if I can book two seats on the Paris plane.'

'Why?' she asked bluntly.

'You need clothes, don't you?'

'Yes, but——'

'And you trust me.' It was a statement, not a question.

'Yes, but——'

'Please stop saying "yes, but"—it gets rather repetitious.'

'Well, you must admit you're a man of surprises!' she snapped, irritated by his tone—and he laughed.

'Yes, I am.'

'And I don't possess a fortune,' she went on. 'I've got precisely one hundred and ten pounds on me. How many clothes do you think *that'll* buy?'

'It won't. You can keep that for pocket money.'

'Hold it a *moment*,' she said. She could see the red telephone kiosk in the distance ahead, but it wasn't for that reason she said the words. 'Just let's get something sorted out.'

'Ah—the telephone. Yes, we'll talk—when I've phoned.' Morgan slowed the car as they neared the kiosk, and pulled on to the verge.

'We'd better talk before,' she said, and he put on the handbrake as he switched off, and looked at her, amused.

'No, after,' he said softly. His dark—nearly black—eyes glinted with laughter, and Sara felt an irrepressible surge of temper.

'Listen,' she snapped. 'I know you "rescued" me from my ghastly aunt's clutches—for which I've already thanked you. But it doesn't give you the right to take charge of me. You've not bought me, you know, so don't——'

He silenced her by putting his hand on her chin and tilting her face up slightly. His hand was large, strong and cool. 'My, my,' he said softly, 'but there's a temper for you! No, I've not bought you, as you so rightly say, but I am going to phone—*now*—and when I come back I'll tell you why we're going to Paris. Right?' He removed the keys from the ignition and put them in his jeans pocket. 'Just in case you have any ideas about driving away. Back in a moment.'

Sara watched him stride away and open the telephone box door. Seething, she sat there. The arrogance of the man! She didn't know why she felt so disturbed, but she did. She was too independent-minded to want *him* to buy her clothes—as he apparently intended to do. A holiday in the South of France, to repay a debt of honour he felt strongly about, was one thing, but taking her to Paris was quite another.

She sat tapping her handbag, smouldering, and watched him emerge a few minutes later.

'All set. We should be there in half an hour—we'll be in good time to change your money before we collect the tickets. Now, you were saying?'

'You know damned well what I was saying! I'm not letting you buy me expensive clothes——'

'Ah, but you'll need them if you're working for me, won't you?'

'I doubt I will, after this,' she answered. 'I'm not even sure I want to come at all.'

His laughter stopped her. It was a shocking intrusion on her indignation. 'Of course you do. You'd kick yourself if you didn't, and you know it, Sara, so don't pretend.'

'How the hell do you know?' she breathed, and glared at him. 'You don't know *me*.'

'Oh, but I do,' he said softly, and in such a way that she felt herself go very still, very quiet—almost shocked.

'What—do you mean?' she whispered.

'I mean that my father used to speak of your father very often—and he emerged as a man who, like my father, enjoyed the sheer exhilaration of living. They spent several dangerous months working together—and in those conditions, got to know each other well, in a way that would probably take years in peacetime. Your father was a courageous man, an adventurer in a world that was full of horror and sadness—and if I'm not mistaken, you've taken after him.' He stopped, and Sara was very still. She was fighting back the tears at this unexpected word picture of her beloved father that Morgan had just painted. And she knew, not only that every word was true, but that she herself was the same. Despite the traumas of the last fortnight, she had only lost her spirit once, when she had cried out in despair in her bedroom—but then fought back. Morgan was more right than he knew. He was probably also a shrewd psychologist, but also, probably, well aware of that fact.

'How do you know that?' she asked quietly, and blinked the tears away before she looked at him.

'How? I saw the way you erupted into that dining room and flung the key on the table, remember. If anyone had the light of battle in her eyes, it was you. And it was at that moment I knew what I was going to ask of you.'

'Right then?'

'Yes. Had I arrived to see you happily settled in with loving relatives, I would have offered you the money that my father would have wished you to have—a gift, you understand, to buy for yourself and your relatives some special surprise—and I would have left, after first giving you my address and making you promise to contact me if ever you needed anything.'

'I see.' She was still shaken. Everything was so cut and dried—organised. But there was something Morgan had just said—what was it? She frowned. Then it came. He had said—'and it was at that moment I knew what I was going to ask of you'—and there had been something extra in the words—she turned to him, and repeated them, and added:

'What are you going to ask of me? It's something connected with Paris, isn't it? It isn't just a holiday you're offering me.'

'And shrewd too. No, you're right.' His face was hard, and he wasn't smiling. 'I would like your help.'

'*You* want *my* help!' she echoed, disbelieving. 'I wouldn't have thought you'd be the man to ask help from anyone—not after seeing the demolition job you did on Aunt Rachel and Elizabeth.'

'This is more—delicate,' he explained. 'And if we don't drive now we'll miss that plane. I'll tell you as we go.' He started the car, then he began to tell her, and Sara listened in growing disbelief. . . .

Now, on the plane, seeing the sea far below, glinting in

the evening sun, she collected her thoughts—and wondered
if she were mad. Because she had agreed to his preposterous
plan. How he had persuaded her she no longer knew, but
it was a fact. He had.

She was going to Paris to be dressed in couture clothes,
and have her long hair styled, and to have an engagement
ring bought for her—and she was going to arrive at the
Villa Esterel as Morgan Haldane's fiancée.

They had adjoining rooms in a hotel off the Champs-
Elysées, and the porter who carried her battered suitcase
upstairs had a knowing smile on his face as he bowed and
left her. Sara glared at the closed door, heard the one opening next to hers, and a moment later Morgan tapped on the
one connecting the two bedrooms. She unbolted it and
stared at him. 'That porter clearly thought I was some
floozie you'd picked up!' she snapped.

He laughed. 'Wait until he sees you depart,' he said.
'He'll have even more of an eye-opener, won't he?'

She hadn't thought of that. She looked down at the
simple cotton dress she wore, and smiled. 'I suppose so.'
Then she glanced at him. 'I'm not sure this is right,' she
said. 'I've been thinking——'

'That's fatal on an empty stomach,' he said. 'And I don't
consider that plastic salad we ate on the plane as food. I'm
going to order dinner to be sent up. We'll eat here, and
we'll go over everything again.'

She nodded. 'Very well. Let me wash, will you?'

'Of course. I'll knock when it arrives.' Morgan went out
silently and Sara locked the door after him. The room was
luxurious, thickly carpeted, the bed large and comfortable-
looking, two easy chairs, a small table, and a tiny bathroom
leading off in one corner. She went over to the window and
looked out at the glittering traffic nosing down the Champs-
Elysées in the distance. Four hours ago she had been
locked in her room with nothing to look forward to except

more arguments with her shrill-voiced aunt and cousins. In minutes, Morgan Haldane had turned her world upside down—and now she was here, and she wasn't sure if she believed it.

She blinked, but the room was still there, as were the muted traffic noises. She opened the window slightly and the sound rushed in, a cacophony. It was somehow reassuring. She had never been to Paris, never been abroad at all, before. Her father had promised her, one day, but it had never materialised. She had got a passport two years previously when it had seemed as if at last they would manage a short holiday in Paris—but the day before, her father had been taken ill, the illness that had led eventually to his death, and her passport had remained untouched since then. Strange, now, that she should be here with it, and with the man he had appealed to, indirectly, for help. . . . She traced a pattern on the window where her breath had steamed the glass. She had cried out in her anguish to her father, and within minutes almost her plea had been answered. She smiled a little smile to herself. Perhaps, somewhere, he already knew. . . .

It was time to wash. She went into the bathroom and ran the water into the bowl. As she was drying her face, she heard Morgan's knock on the communicating door. 'I'm coming now,' she answered, went across, unbolted it, and went into his room.

A meal was set on the table, and beside it a loaded trolley with covered dishes. 'I like my food,' said Morgan. 'I hope you do too. I don't know your tastes, so I've ordered simple fare, onion soup followed by chicken—and the speciality sweet of this hotel, crème caramel.'

'Sounds delicious to me,' she murmured. 'And I'm starving.'

'Good.' He pulled a chair out for her. 'And we can talk as we eat.'

There was a bottle of wine on the table, and he poured

out two glasses. '*Bon appetit*,' he said.

'*Merci. Et vous aussi.*'

'Ah. You speak French?'

'Enough to get by.'

'Good. A bonus. My housekeeper is French and the best cook on the Riviera, but she refuses to learn English. You'll be able to communicate well.'

'I hope so,' said Sara. 'You'd better tell me the set up at the villa, hadn't you?'

'Of course. Apart from Martine—the housekeeper— there's her husband, Jacques, and their son Marc, who garden for me. A couple of cleaners come twice a week.'

'And the—the woman who is the reason for me being engaged to you—where does she fit in?'

'Louise?' He laughed. 'She's the next-door neighbour. She and her husband.'

'What?' she spluttered over a mouthful of soup. 'She's *married*! You didn't say *that*!'

'Would it make any difference if I had?' he answered, eyes narrowing.

'Yes, it damned well would!' she retorted. 'It seemed odd to start with that you should be so bothered about some woman—I mean, *you*!—but to know she's married as well! That's ridiculous!'

'Is it?' he said levelly. 'Then I can see I haven't told you enough. I'd better start the story properly. Keep eating.'

Seething, confused, Sara spooned her soup up, and he began to speak.

'Louise's husband is Jack Barron, a business partner of mine. He's a lot older than her, about sixty. Louise admits to thirty-one—but you'll see how true that is when you meet her. They've been married for ten years, and as far as I know she's had a string of lovers since then. Jack either doesn't know, or mind, because he's so besotted with her that she can do no wrong. She's a perfect bitch, and if I were him I'd have sent her packing years ago, but I'm not him. I am, however, very fond of him. We're partners in a couple of restaurants on the French Riviera—and I want nothing to spoil that. Louise wants an affair with me; I may be putting it bluntly, but I know no other way. She's made it quite clear, over the last six months or so, that she would like to get me to bed, and I can do without complications of that sort in my private or business life. I've always left married women strictly alone——'

'Just a moment,' said Sara calmly. 'Where, pray, do *I* fit into this little charade?'

'I would have thought it obvious. She can hardly keep waylaying me the minute Jack goes off somewhere if you're around, can she?'

Sara put her empty soup plate to one side. 'She's obviously a sophisticated woman, right?' He nodded. 'And she "admits" as you put it, to thirty-one—so let's say she's thirty-five, for the sake of argument. Do you honestly think a clever, sophisticated woman like that is going to be deterred by *me*?' She waved her arm to indicate her hair and her dress. 'Thanks for the compliment,' she said wryly, 'but no, thanks.'

'You underestimate yourself,' answered Morgan, equally wry in tone. 'I told you, you're your father's daughter. You have the advantage of years over her—you're taller, slightly slimmer, and you were a match for that ghastly aunt and cousin of yours.'

'They weren't rivals for your affections,' she retorted smartly. 'I'm nineteen, nearly twenty, I've never had a boy-friend or a job, I was too busy nursing my father to think about either, and I've no tricks up my sleeve at all.'

'Then be yourself,' he said quietly.

'Hah! What's she like?'

'A natural blonde, green eyes, slightly slanting, classical features—she's an actress, or was a few years ago, very exotic, dresses in stunning clothes——'

'Do you fancy her?'

'No.'

She gave him a level look. 'I believe you.'

'Thank you.' Sara felt herself redden at the sarcasm.

'Have you got a girl-friend?' she asked.

He gave a thin smile. 'Why do you ask?'

'I would have thought it obvious,' she said, copying his words of a few moments before. 'You could have asked her instead.'

He said nothing, and, annoyed, she said: 'Couldn't you?'

'I'm a normal man—I have women friends——'

'You haven't answered my question yet.'

His eyes narrowed. 'Nor do I intend to.'

Her temper flared. 'You ask *me* to pretend to be your fiancée, and I'm not even supposed to know if there's a jealous woman somewhere glaring daggers at me! Thanks!'

'You'll cope,' he assured her.

'Hah!'

'Would you rather be at Aunty's?' he asked drily.

'No! And if *you* hadn't turned up I'd be at the Y.W.C.A.'

'With all due respect to the Y.W.C.A., I think you'll find life at the villa more interesting.'

'Oh, *sure*,' she answered with heavy irony. 'And how long does the little charade last, pray?'

'Until she realises she's not getting anywhere and finds herself another lover. The Riviera is teeming with lusty young men, a lot of them very wealthy, who'll be only too happy to oblige.'

'And then what? Do I leave you and go back to England?'

'Not if you don't want to. I told you, I can give you a good job.'

'I thought this—this engagement was the good job.'

'Oh no, Sara. I have a hotel as well, in Cannes. You can work there if you want as receptionist, or secretary, or whatever you choose.'

'Just like that?' she stared at him, wide-eyed. Hotel

owner, restaurateur—what else?

'Yes.'

'Are those all your business interests?' she asked.

'No. There's something else.' He stood up and uncovered the dishes.

'What is it?' she asked, intrigued by something in his voice.

'I'll show you when we're there.'

'Why not now?'

'Because.'

Morgan was filling her plate with luscious-looking chicken, and her mouth watered. She felt vaguely angry with him, with the manipulation he had skilfully performed on her, but she couldn't put into words what she wanted to say. 'Is that enough for you?' he asked.

'Yes, fine. Look, Morgan——' she began.

He sighed. 'Can't we eat?'

'Are you like this with everybody?' she snapped.

He raised one eyebrow, dark eyes very level—hard. 'Like what?'

'Manipulating them! Getting your own way—talking when it suits you and then—shut people up?'

'Very possibly,' he said, which infuriated her more. She glared at her plate.

'Huh. Pity I hadn't left before you arrived,' she muttered.

She was startled by a noise and looked up to see him turning aside, spluttering into his serviette. He was laughing—actually laughing at her! It was the last straw. Incensed, Sara stood up, picked up her plate, and flung it at him. She watched the pieces of chicken and gravy slowly fall down the sweater, and her heart bumped in horror at what she had done, but it was too late. As Morgan wiped the food from him, she turned and fled into her room and slammed it shut. As she fumbled for the bolt the door crashed open and he came in, ripping off his pullover as he kicked the door back, and Sara thought, for one blinding

instant, that he intended to rape her. She saw the expression
on his face, the narrowed eyes, the hawklike features, a deep
rage in every line, and she was mortally afraid, and backed,
turning, seeking escape——

He caught hold of her, swung her round, and pulled her
to him. She saw the hard planes of his face, saw for an un-
forgettable instant, the legacy of his American Indian
blood before everything was blotted out as his mouth
came down on hers, hard and savage in a punishing kiss
that hurt and excited her all at the same time. She had
never been kissed before. She had wondered what her first
kiss would be like, but had never imagined anything like this.
Vainly she struggled to free herself, hating herself, hating
him—her breath almost knocked out of her body as she
fought—and then, suddenly it changed. For a moment Morgan paused, moved—then he kissed her again, and this time
it was the kiss she had imagined in her dreams. It was a kiss
so sensual and warming that she felt the hairs prickle on the
back of her neck, and the tingle along her spine, followed by
his hand as he ran it down her back, to her waist, and
pressed her closer to him. His breath was sweet, his mouth
sweeter, and sensual and exciting, and it all mingled into one
sensation of being out of the world, not part of it any longer,
but floating...floating away....

He released her abruptly and she felt her legs give way. He
caught her as she would have fallen, and held her to him
again, and she could feel the pulsing beat of his heart against
her breast. She could feel the bare skin of him against her,
hard, muscular bare skin, very tanned, and the arms that held
her were equally strong and brown.

'I'm—sorry,' she whispered. 'I shouldn't have done what I
did.' She could think of nothing else to say. Her head still
reeled from the impact of his brief lovemaking, and she was
trembling. 'But you shouldn't have—k-kissed me like
that——'

Morgan looked down at her, eyes so dark, so very dark.

'It was either that or beat you,' he said.

'I was—frightened,' she said, so quietly that he had to bend his head to hear.

'Can you stand?' he asked.

'Yes, I think so.' He took his hands away, slowly, as if ready to catch her should she sway, then he looked at her.

'You may as well know, I have a temper to match yours, Sara. I don't want to fight you—but if you ever do anything again like that, I will.'

'Is that how you fight women?' she whispered, a spark of scorn in her eyes.

He smiled thinly. 'It's the only way I know. I don't hit women, if that's what you mean.'

She picked up the stained sweater. 'I'll wash this and put it to dry on the radiator. Please—leave me.'

Without another word he walked out. Sara put her fingers to her lips. She should hate him for what he had done, but she didn't. She suddenly realised he fascinated her. She wanted him to kiss her again.

CHAPTER THREE

SARA bolted the door, then went to wash the black sweater in her bathroom. She rolled it up in the bath towel, then spread it over the warm radiator to dry. A knock came at the connecting door. 'Sara?'

'What do you want?' She stared at the door wide-eyed. She didn't want Morgan to come in, and she didn't want him not to come in. She didn't know what she wanted, except that he had awakened a powerful response in her that she hadn't known existed.

'I've given you the chicken that was left in the dish, and some vegetables.'

She was still hungry. She deeply regretted her impulsive temper. She went and unbolted the door and he stood there holding a plate.

'What about you?' she asked.

'I'll have some vegetables—there's enough for me. Eat.'

'Thank you.' The storm had gone, leaving in its wake the calm. Sara felt drained of all emotion. She wanted to cry. She wanted Morgan to hold her and comfort her, only he couldn't know that, and he wouldn't if he did; he would probably laugh. He nodded.

'Goodnight, Sara, sleep well. I'll see you in the morning.' He was gone. She bolted the door, went to stand by the window and ate as she looked out over the darkened city with the lights glistening blurrily in the sudden shower of rain that had started. She was confused and jumpy, her nerve ends ragged with shock. Six hours previously she hadn't even known that men like Morgan Haldane existed, save perhaps in films. And now she was his official 'fiancée', they had had a brief tempestuous fight—and he had kissed

34

her. As an alternative to a beating, he had said, and she could imagine the truth of that. She shivered, a delicious trembling that suffused her body and made her go warm. Dear Lord, she thought, what would he be like when he made love? Her heart beat erratically, and she put the plate down at her side and leaned her forehead against the cool glass, as she had done not so many hours ago in her attic bedroom, then in despair—and now—for a different reason. Morgan Haldane was a man of power, a tough ruthless man, dark and strong. He was repaying a debt of honour—but he was also using her, she knew she mustn't forget that. He had seen the way she had behaved at her aunt's house—and he had decided, in an instant, that she could help him.

So be it, she thought. I'll accept that, because whatever kind of man he is, he has brought me from that house, and I'll have no worries about job hunting, not for a while anyway. She lifted her head proudly. The future could take care of itself. The next month or so was what was important now. She would think of herself as Morgan's fiancée until that time came when the charade would be over, and then she would leave. She turned away from the window and looked at the closed adjoining door. She saw his face as it had been in those few seconds of pursuit, the narrowed eyes, the hawklike features—the rage—and her heart bumped. He had been potentially dangerous, a jungle beast after its prey—for a few moments the mask of civilisation had slipped and she had seen the primitive man behind it. And what had he said? 'You may as well know now, I have a temper to match yours, Sara.' He was wrong; his was far more devastating. She had felt the absolute strength of him when he had kissed her—the first a punishment, savage, brutal, the second—ah! different. So very different, a world apart from that first one. He was a man of sensuality, of deep passion and excitement, and Sara could understand the faithless wife of his neighbour lusting after him—and his concern about it. She wondered, wryly, whether he would be so concerned if Louise were not married to a business partner. He had said that he left married women strictly alone—but that might have been to allay her suspicions. . . .

She shivered, not so warm now, remembering his touch, the way her pulses had leapt in instinctive response. Morgan was a dangerous man to know, and yet his father and her father had been linked in a most difficult time in the past, and that link reached out and bound them now. Helplessly she moved away, hands clenched together. It must be made clear to him now—she must make it very plain— but how? She bit her lip. How did you say to a man like him that it was an engagement in name only? Suppose he laughed and said—what else? as if the idea that he might want to make love to her was too absurd for words? Sara wasn't sophisticated. She had already told him that she knew no feminine guiles and he had told her to be herself —but that was in regard to Louise. Suppose he——

She walked forward, about to tap the door and beard the lion in his den—but was startled by the sharp rapping that came from the other side as she lifted her hand.

'Yes?' she asked, heart thudding.

'Sara, can I have a word with you?'

'Just a moment.' She unbolted the door and opened it. 'I was just about to say the same,' she began.

Morgan walked in. 'Then fire away,' he answered.

She cleared her throat. 'I—er—I've been thinking about things,' she said. 'Um—you'd better sit down.'

He had put on a white shirt, not tucked in, and without a tie, and he regarded her quizzically but went and sat down without saying another word.

'Ahem——' she cleared her throat again. 'I—er—this is very difficult,' she began, then stopped, mind horrifyingly blank. She could only look at him in dismay.

'Perhaps I can help?' he said drily. 'Is it something to do with our recent "fight"—and the fact that you're going to be, to all intents and purposes, my fiancée?'

'Yes,' she said in a whisper.

'And that's what I was coming to talk to you about.' He regarded her levelly, eyes very dark, almost black, unfathomable. 'You're worried that the little act of ours might spill over into whatever private life we have?'

'Yes,' she nodded.

He stood up, then looked her up and down, slowly. She could almost feel the black, black eyes touching every inch of her. She gazed back at his almost defiantly.

'You're safe,' he said. 'As safe as you want to be. Does that answer your question, Sara?'

She swallowed. It didn't, but how could she tell him? How could she say that he had awakened something she hadn't even known existed, within herself?

'Yes,' she said. He was clever too. For the first time she wondered if she was playing with fire by being with him. Too late now, she was committed. A frisson of excitement shivered down her spine.

'Good.' He walked towards her. 'And now, having cleared the air, are you ready to go to bed—or do you want to go out and sample the night life of gay Paree?'

Sara looked down at her dress. 'Like this?'

He shrugged. 'Like anything you want. It's only eleven. I know a little night club not far away—we could stay an hour, no more. I promise you'll find it interesting.'

It was a challenge, and she never refused a challenge. 'You're on,' she said. 'I've a long skirt in my case. Give me two minutes to change.'

'Knock when you're ready. I'll phone down for a taxi—it's raining.' She watched him go, opened her case and found the one and only long black skirt she possessed. It was simple, she had made it herself a year or so previously, and rolled up with it was a black cotton sweater, round-necked, long-sleeved. She stripped and put them on, then looked in the mirror. The effect, she was pleased to note, was one of

slender elegance. If only she had a necklace or pendant to
wear with it! She sighed, laughed at her vanity, and went to
knock on the adjoining door.

'Come in.' Morgan put his telephone down as she went in,
turned, and looked at her. 'That's fine,' he said, in some surprise.

'Hm, it'd be nicer if I'd some jewellery to wear,' she
answered. 'Never mind, I won't feel out of place in a night-
club. Are you ready?'

He put on a black jacket, and she saw that he had already
put on a dark blue tie. He looked quite formally dressed. She
felt suddenly happy for the first time in weeks, and smiled.
She was going out with an attractive man, in Paris, the city of
lovers, and tomorrow she would be in the South of France.
Little Mendover, her aunt and cousins, and a dismal attic
bedroom, suddenly seemed far away.

'I'm ready,' he answered. 'The taxi will be waiting. Let's
go.'

He locked the door, pocketed the key, and they took the
elevator down to the well lit foyer, not crowded, but not empty
either, with tourists, mainly American, milling round and
talking. 'Just a moment,' said Morgan, and went over to the
reception clerk and spoke quietly to him. Sara, standing a few
feet away, couldn't hear what was being said, but she saw
Morgan point, saw the clerk shake his head, and she looked in
the direction of Morgan's hand—and went very still. He had
pointed to a case in the foyer, that was well lit, and clearly a
display case for jewellery from some Parisian store. Had he
thought she was *hinting*? There was a brief discussion, a regretful shaking of head and a Gallic shrug from the man at
reception—then some notes changed hands, and the regretful
head-shake turned into an equally Gallic nod, and an expan-
sive beam. Sara smiled to herself. When Morgan said her
name, quietly, she went over to him.

'Look, I didn't mean——' she began.

'I know.' He regarded her very levelly, very shrewdly. 'I

don't think you have it in you to drop hints. But allow me to buy you a small present—a token, if you like.'

The case was opened. The display was dazzling, and a few women guests wandered nearer, ever so casually, but looking, smiling. There was a pendant on a heavy silver chain. It was a teardrop-shaped piece of jade, delicately carved with flower patterns. Morgan lifted it out and held it against Sara's sweater. 'Like it?' he asked.

'Mmm!' she sighed. It was beautiful. But how much was it? There were no prices shown.

'Then let's try it on.' She felt cool fingers at the back of her neck, a click, and it was on. She touched it, looked in a nearby mirror. It was beautiful. 'Stay there,' he said, and walked back to the desk with the clerk. She saw him writing a cheque, then he was following her out, taking her arm. 'Let's go,' he said, and she saw the taxi waiting, its engine running. Another man was talking to the driver, leaning in. Morgan went, spoke to the driver, nodded pleasantly to the man, and opened the door for Sara.

The man, an American, was drunk. 'Hey,' he said, 'just a minute, bud——'

Morgan looked at him. '*I* ordered this taxi,' he said quietly, and Sara saw his face, saw the hard eyes, very dark, that met the American's, and shivered. There was no compromise there, none at all. There was no aggression either, just the look of a man who was well aware that he was in the right and wasn't prepared to argue about it. It hit the American with the force of a wave, and he stepped back, muttered something, and turned away, pulling a disgusted face.

Sara got in. Morgan spoke to the driver and they were off, weaving swiftly through traffic. She looked at him. 'Is that how you deal with any opposition?' she asked.

He looked back at her blankly. 'What?'

'The drunk.'

'Oh, him.' He smiled. 'That was hardly opposition, Sara.

It was our taxi. What would you have had me done? Let him take it?'

'No, but—you *looked* at him—I saw it.'

'So?' He laughed. 'Did you expect me to punch him? That's not the way I work—as you'll see.'

Yes, she thought, I'm sure I will. She looked down at her sweater, touched the pendant. 'Thank you very much for this,' she said. 'It's beautiful.'

'I'm happy you like it. Have you ever been to a night club before?'

It was her turn to laugh. 'Do I look as though I have? No, I've led a very quiet life up until now.'

The taxi was slowing, entering a side street filled with parked cars. It was a dark street, but at the end a bright neon sign proclaimed the word: 'Georges.'

'Nearly there.' Morgan touched her hand briefly. 'You'll find it interesting.'

'I'm sure I will.' He helped her out, and paid the driver, who grinned, presumably at a fair tip, and wished them a good night. Sara watched him drive away, then looked at the closed door ahead of them. There was a glass porthole in it, and she swallowed. *This* was a night club? Morgan saw her face, rapped on the door, looked down at her. 'They don't let just anyone in,' he said softly. 'You wouldn't want to go somewhere full of drunks, would you?'

She shook her head, saw a face peer out, then the door opened and a very large man, as dark and tall as Morgan but twice as broad, was standing there beaming at them. He embraced Morgan, gold teeth flashing, eyes delighted.

'Monsieur Haldane—*bienvenu*! *Et vous, madame!*'

'Hello, Georges,' Morgan grinned at the man. 'My friend Miss Bourne wants to sample Parisian night life—so naturally I brought her here.'

'But of course!' Georges' English was delightfully fractured. He gave Sara the benefit of the gold teeth, which nearly dazzled her, and shook her hand, bowing low over it. 'You are most welcome, Mees Bourne. Any friend of M'sieur Haldane is *most* welcome here. *Bien!* Follow me, please.' He led them down red-carpeted stairs into a narrow passage. Noise pulsed from the door at the end, and flooded out as he opened it. They were in a large, dimly lit room, with tables round the circle of dance floor that was crammed with people dancing to the music of a small band on a stage.

As her eyes became accustomed to the dim light, Sara could see that each table had a lit candle in a bottle, that the tables were crammed with glasses, that everyone seemed to be having a wonderful time. The air was heavy with smoke and perfume. George weaved a skilful way through to a table in the corner, and deftly whipped several empty glasses from it. 'Your usual?' he enquired, and Morgan nodded.

They sat down. Several women had turned their heads at Morgan's entrance, and some remained looking, discreetly, so that their companions wouldn't see. Sara blinked, the smoke an irritation, the noise deafening, and Morgan leaned over and said: 'You'll get used to the noise in a few minutes.'

'Will I?' she laughed. 'It's—fascinating. Do you come here often?'

'About once a year. Georges was a friend of my father's in the war—he's over sixty, though he doesn't look it—and he was a great Resistance worker. You wouldn't believe it to look at him now, but he used to be known as the Weasel, he was as skinny as a beanpole, and could move as swiftly as my father. He knew your father as well, Sara.'

'Oh.' She saw Georges returning with a waiter, a slim dark youth carrying a bucket with a champagne bottle nestling in ice. The bucket was placed with due ceremony on a stand beside their table, and Georges opened it as the waiter darted off. She looked at him with new respect. This man knew her father. Perhaps, if he hadn't been taken ill, and they had come, they might have found this place.

He filled their glasses, and Morgan began speaking to him, telling him, as far as Sara was able to follow the conversation in that noise, who she was. She saw Georges' face change, saw him look at her, then he pulled up a chair beside her and took her hand. As the waiter returned with a tray of small dishes filled with olives, nuts, and crisps, he said something to him, and the waiter darted away again.

'My dear,' he said, and she was astounded to see tears filling his eyes. 'My dear, what can I say? I knew your father, Philip'—he pronounced it in the French way, as Philippe—'so well. He and Red Haldane were two of the finest men I ever met. I cannot tell you how honoured I am to have met you.' Raising his voice so that Morgan could hear as well, he said, 'You are both my honoured guests to-night——' and as the waiter returned, with another glass, he said: '*Plus de champagne*, Michel.' He turned back to them both. 'I insist on drinking your good health—and anything you wish, *anything*, it is yours.' They raised their glasses. Sara had never tasted champagne before. It was sharp, cool, delicious—and tingled up her nose, nearly making her gasp.

'*Votre santé, mes chers!*' Georges announced, the tears brimming in his eyes, in no way looking out of place. Bemused, dazed, Sara drank, and allowed him to fill her glass again. She looked across at Morgan who was watching them both with a calm, slightly amused expression on his face, and suddenly felt very happy, ridiculously, absurdly happy. She wanted to cry and to laugh at the same moment.

'*Merci*, Monsieur Georges,' she responded. 'I'd love to dance.' And she laughed. He joined in.

'Dance?' You wish me to clear the floor for you and Morgan? *Eh voilà*—it shall be done!'

'Oh no,' she said, alarmed, and put her hand on his arm as he would have stood. 'I mean—*with* the crowd. Is it disco music?' The sounds blared out as if in confirmation, and the dancers writhed and gestured, not touching each other, each one in a world of their own.

Georges pulled a face. '*Hélas*, yes,' he admitted. 'It is all the rage, you see. No more old-fashioned waltzes.' He patted his ample stomach. '*Et moi, hélas*, I can no longer dance as I used to.'' He laughed hugely, enjoying himself, 'or I would ask you, *mademoiselle*!'

Morgan stood. 'You want to dance, Sara? Right.' To Georges he said: 'We won't be long. I think I'm too old for this myself. Keep the champagne cool, Georges—we'll be back.' He put his hand under Sara's elbow and steered her towards the noise.

She felt a moment of dismay as she saw the contortions performed on the floor. It was an evening of firsts for her. Paris—night club—now this. She looked at the man waiting by her side at the edge of the crowded floor.

'I'm not too sure myself,' she shouted, so that he would hear, and he laughed.

'Serve you right! Okay, let's take the plunge. I'll try not to disgrace you,' and he pulled her on to the floor, casting his eyes round swiftly, assessingly, and began to move in a similar fashion.

Within moments they had it. There was a natural rhythm to the music, and an infectious atmosphere that lent itself to imitation, and Sara found herself enjoying it immensely. Morgan was lithe and light on his feet, and moved sensually and sinuously to the beat of the drums, and Sara, younger, naturally agile, was lost in the world of noise and colour and pulsing excitement.

When they returned after several hectic dances to the table, Georges was waiting, and he applauded them enthusiastically. '*Merveilleux!*' he exclaimed. 'I watched you. Ah, beautiful!' He handed Sara a glass full of champagne. 'Drink, my dear, *mademoiselle*, and you, Morgan.'

Things began to get blurred after that, but beautifully so. She was aware of Georges vanishing, to return with platefuls of a delicious seafood concoction which he insisted they eat—as his honoured guests. Then more champagne, more noise, colour, a cabaret, light blurring, the candle sparkling and spluttering, people greeting Georges, couples passing, laughing, more champagne....

It seemed a blissful eternity had passed when at last they were bidding Georges goodnight at the door. Sara felt as if she were walking on air, and looked down, puzzled. The ground was solid enough. The rain had stopped and the air was faintly warm, and in the sky the first light of dawn chased the darkness away. Georges kissed her cheeks warmly, then embraced Morgan. 'You will come again soon,' he begged. 'You will not leave it so long, hey?'

'I promise, Georges,' Morgan smiled.

'But you must let me call you a taxi! To walk back, I cannot allow it!'

'I think we could both do with the fresh air,' Morgan responded. 'It's nearly five'—good grief, thought Sara bemused, is it?—'and it's not far. Thank you for an excellent evening, Georges. You are the perfect host.'

'From you I take that as a superb compliment,' Georges tried to smile modestly, not quite succeeding. 'But give me notice next time, hey? And you will not be disappointed.' He looked at Sara, the tears springing to his eyes as he did so. 'And you, little English mees, you come with him too, hey? For me? For old times' sake?'

'I will,' she promised. She would have promised him anything at the moment; the world was a wonderful place. She kissed his cheek gently. 'Thank you, Georges, I've enjoyed myself very much.'

'Ah, I am so very happy to have met you. *Au revoir*, Sara.'

He watched them go, and when they reached the end of the narrow street, Sara looked back. He was standing on the pavement. He blew a kiss and waved, and she waved back, and so did Morgan.

There was no traffic about, and she danced along the

empty pavement, smelling the fresh damp air, drinking in the scents of Paris, and it was like nowhere else in the world. She lifted her arms and looked up at the lightening sky, faintly pink, then laughed and looked round at the man walking behind her, his expression amused.

'I'm not drunk,' she said, faintly annoyed by the slight smile.

'Of course not,' he said. 'Did I say you were?' He paused to light a small cigar, and the smoke wreathed round his head, and he caught up with her.

'But you're laughing,' she accused.

'No, I'm not. I have had a very pleasant evening at Georges', and I've just realised that I didn't intend to stay more than two hours, and we were there nearly six—that's why I'm smiling.'

Sara whirled round and nearly stumbled, and he caught her arm and steadied her. 'Careful,' he warned. 'I know you're perfectly sober, but just remember you've drunk quite a fair amount of champagne.'

'So?' she laughed. 'It's very pleasant.'

'I know. It's also not lemonade. I should have got him to bring you a black coffee before we left.'

'Hah! There's nothing wrong with——' and then she stopped, because the world whirred round. The fresh air had hit her, belatedly. She felt very dizzy, and gasped. Morgan held her to him.

'Steady now,' he said softly, and flicked his cigar away.

'Oh!' she leant against his chest. 'Oh, Morgan——' She closed her eyes, feeling the steady beat of his heart against her head, which was suddenly filled with whirling lights.

'I know,' he soothed. 'Want me to get a taxi? There's a phone——'

'No,' her voice was muffled, 'I'd rather walk.' She felt herself being led gently, then they were in a shop doorway. It was an expensive looking clothes shop, the windows still lit. He held her.

'Stay still a few moments,' he said, 'then we'll walk.

When you're ready.' His arms were very steady and strong around her, and she could feel the strength of them, very gentle too, and her heart was so full that it seemed that it might burst, and she looked up at him, helpless, vulnerable, suddenly very aware of his nearness. He looked down at her at the same moment, and his face was very close, and clear in the light from the window. She could see his tanned skin, his dark unfathomable eyes, regarding her seriously, she could see the dark shadow of his beard, see his mouth, that wide sensual mouth that she had known so well, so briefly; and softly, almost unaware of what she was doing, she lifted her mouth to his, standing on tiptoe, and kissed him.

The world whirled round again as she clung to him, lost to everything except the sensation of what was happening. For a brief moment his lips remained cool, then he responded—and now it was no longer Sara kissing him, it was Morgan kissing her. She heard a murmur, and it could have been him, or it could have been her, she didn't know, and it didn't matter. The kiss was warm, deep and wonderful; his hands caressed her back lightly, delicious soft touches along her spine, filling her with such warmth that she knew, now, that this was how she had known all along that the evening would end. In his arms. . . .

His hold on her tightened imperceptibly. She had her back to the shop door, although she hadn't been aware of them moving round. Her head and body were filled with light and fire and a shivering ecstasy she had never known could exist. If he let go of her she would fall, but he didn't. She felt as if her life was passing through her mind, the quiet years, the growing up, the time passing in a kaleidoscopic whirl of colour and tone, and all leading up, inevitably to this moment on a Parisian pavement, in a quiet secluded doorway, all leading to this. . . .

She pulled him towards her, knowing the hardness of his body against her was all she had ever wanted, sensually delighting in the hard lean length of him against her, and she moved, gently blurring her body against his, revelling in her senses.

'Sara,' he murmured, his voice very soft, 'you're doing things to me you shouldn't be doing——' soft, but it held dismay mingled with delight, and some amusement, and something else, as if he had to make a token protest. Sara caught the amusement, and laughed softly and wriggled herself shamelessly against him, and he groaned. 'For God's sake, Sara——' he began.

She silenced him. She covered his mouth with her own, and she knew she was doing things she would never do, but the champagne was having the most devastating effect on her, and so it didn't seem to matter any more. . . .

Then it was all over. For Morgan pulled himself away, and it seemed that it had been an effort for him, and he looked down at her, and his eyes were very bright and dark upon her, and she could see the faint muscle that moved at the corner of his mouth as he said: 'We'd better go.' His voice no longer held amusement. She thought she must be imagining that he seemed almost angry. The spell was broken, shattered by what was in his face, and she felt suddenly icily sober. She shuddered. Oh God! What had happened? The world no longer whirled round. It was very still, and hushed, as if it too waited for him to speak. Sara wanted to say, don't be angry, don't look at me like that—but she couldn't. She shivered and hugged her arms, cold. Morgan had been amused, and now he was no longer amused—and she knew why. She had flung herself on him abandonedly, because the champagne she had drunk had made the world seem a wonderful place and she had had a wonderful evening—only now it was over. She had behaved like the child she was, immature and unsophisticated. Louise wouldn't have behaved like that, she would have been more subtle. She turned her head away, unable to look at him any more, and looked into the window, seeing the dresses there blurred with her tears. She swallowed.

'I'm sorry,' she said. She despised herself—and she despised him. He could have done it more gently, not that slap in the face his cold words had been: 'We'd better go.' Contempt in every word. She looked at him then, after taking a deep breath to give her courage.

'Yes, we'd better go,' she said. 'Blame the drink—I'm not used to it, as you may have gathered.'

'I know.' He reached out to touch her arm, but she wrenched it free.

'Please don't touch me,' she breathed. 'I've sobered up quite suddenly, I don't need any help.' Her mouth felt very stiff, but she forced the words out. 'Let's walk.' She blinked her eyes dry. 'I'm fine now.' That was the biggest lie she had ever told in her life, but as long as he believed it, it would be all right. But he didn't move, he looked at her, and she wanted to scream at him to get out of the way, but she held herself steady instead and stared at him.

'Well?' she said. 'Aren't we going?' She smiled brightly to let him see that it didn't matter—*nothing* mattered, and it had just been a pleasant five minutes' necking to her as well, so why didn't he *see* it? Why was he looking at her like that, all serious, all of a sudden?

'Not like this,' he said. 'Not until we get something straight.'

'Oh, for heaven's sake!' she burst out. 'What's to get straight? I was sloshed—all right, I admit it, I was, and I was brazen enough to kiss you. Big deal! There's no need to look at me as if I'd tried to rape you——' the words died in her throat as she saw his face change. 'Why don't you *move*?' she added fiercely.

'*Did* you know what you were doing?' he asked.

'What *do* you mean?' she said lightly—it was an effort to keep her tone light, but she managed somehow.

'I think you know.'

Something snapped. She whirled on him, arm upraised to

hit him, but he caught it and held it. She tried to pull her hand free, but in vain, and she whispered: 'Let me go, you big brute—and I'm not standing here talking to you, I want to get to bed. It's late—as you reminded me.' She tugged her hand, trying to free it, but he held her with a steel-like grip. 'Damn you,' she breathed. 'Let me *go*!'

'I'm not made of stone, Sara. Thank your lucky stars we were standing in a shop doorway in the open. Had we been somewhere quieter I would have made love to you.'

She caught her breath, shocked at the quiet inexorability of his words. Made love, made love, they seemed to echo, and she suddenly knew the truth of them, and was very still, not struggling any longer, her hand limp in his, her body trembling inwardly. She closed her eyes, and he lifted her chin with his free hand, and she opened her eyes again, caught as if mesmerised in his glance. 'And that's not part of the arrangement, Sara—I'm no saint, but I don't go around seducing young virgins—but there comes a moment——' he paused, as if seeking the words to say what he had to. 'There comes a moment,' he went on, 'when judgment becomes blurred.' He closed his eyes for a moment. 'I shouldn't have to spell it out, should I?'

Sara ran her tongue along her dry lips. 'No,' she whispered. Morgan released her hand, but kept his other one still on her chin, cupping it. His fingers were cool and strong, not gentle, but not rough.

'That was why I—stopped.'

'It won't happen again,' she said, and reached up to push his hand from her chin. 'I'll see to that.' Her eyes were angry, and she blazed at him. 'Now, is the lecture over? Can we go? You're *safe* from me!' She began to laugh, and pushed past him, and began to run down the empty street, and didn't look to see if he was following. She didn't care.

CHAPTER FOUR

SARA lay in her bed. She felt wretched; her head ached, her eyes ached, her throat was sore. She had stripped off her skirt and sweater and tumbled into bed in bra and pants, and fallen straight away into a deep but dream-filled sleep.

She opened her eyes to see the light flooding in, and what had woken her was the knocking on the communicating door. She looked at the door, then turned her head away.

'Sara?' It was Morgan, of course. She didn't want to speak to him, or see him. She felt ashamed and ill.

The door opened slowly, and then she turned her head. She had forgotten to bolt it when she had come in! 'Go away,' she said, as he walked in. He came over to the bed and looked down at her.

'Are you all right?'

She pulled the covers up nearly over her head. 'No. Go away.' She felt the weight on the bed as he sat down, and the next moment the cover was pulled away from her face.

'It's nearly ten o'clock,' he said. 'It's time you were up.'

She knew she was behaving badly, but she felt too wretched to care. She pulled the sheet from him. 'I've telephoned your uncle,' he said, 'to let him know our change of plans. He sends his love.' When she didn't answer he said:

'Did you hear what I said?'

'Yes, thank you.'

'Do you want something for your hangover?'

She fought with the desire to tell him to go to hell or admitting she felt awful, and that won. 'Yes, please.'

The weight moved. 'Okay. I'll not be a minute.' She heard the door close, waited a moment, then got out of bed and went into the bathroom. She locked the door, stripped and had a shower, which made her feel somewhat better. Not much, but slightly. All right, she told herself as she looked in the mirror and cleaned her teeth vigorously, snap out of it, Sara. What are you, a woman or a mouse? Forget what happened—grow up, girl. You've agreed to what you've agreed and you can jolly well do it. She pulled a face at her reflection, winced as her head throbbed in protest, and went back into the bedroom for her clean underwear. She was choosing what to wear from the meagre selection in her case when the knock came at the door.

'Just a moment!' she called, grabbed the sweater she had worn the previous night, and a grey pleated skirt, and put them on. 'Come in.'

Morgan came in carrying a glass. He looked across the room at her, and she met his eyes boldly. It was now or never. Nothing had happened—*nothing*—and she wasn't going to act as if she were ashamed.

'Thank you. If you'll put it down on the table——'

'And these.' He was holding two round white capsules. 'Put them in the water when you're ready and they'll dissolve. Do you want any breakfast?'

'No, thanks. Do you?'

'I've eaten an hour ago. I've been busy making appointments for us. In an hour you're having your hair done, then we're going to buy some clothes, and then a ring.'

Sara smiled, walked across to the table and dropped the two capsules into the glass. She swirled it round and watched them fizz. 'You don't waste time, do you?'

'No, I don't. Will you be ready in an hour?'

'I'm practically ready now, as you see.' She swallowed the bubbling liquid, grimacing at its bitterness. 'Ugh!' she shuddered.

Morgan took the glass from her. 'You've made a quick recovery,' he remarked.

She regarded him coolly. 'Yes.' There was a tension in

the room, reaching out to enfold them both, a subtle under-current beneath his words, and her brief reply.

'Good,' he nodded. He knew all right, he sensed it too, and he was dark and strong and powerful; she remembered his hands, the touch of them on her, and how she had known a brief wonder when he had kissed her, but it wasn't going to happen again because she was out of her depth in some things and she wasn't his type of woman, that was obvious, even if she was going to pretend to be his fiancée. His kind of woman would be cool and sophisti-cated and never do silly things like flinging herself at a man because she'd drunk too much champagne. His kind of woman would be like one she'd noticed staring at him in the night club of Georges', tall, blonde, svelte, clad in a stunningly simple dress of black velvet. Sara had seen Mor-gan's eyes on the woman several times, when he thought Sara had been paying all her attention to Georges, and she had been amused then, and she wondered, fleetingly, if it had been one reason why she had kissed him, afterwards, in that doorway. . . .

He was speaking, and she had to concentrate on his words, had to drag her mind back from the woman who had smiled at him briefly, flirtatiously—and had probably wondered what he was doing with Sara.

'—and we'll fly down this evening. That's arranged as well.'

She nodded coolly. 'Yes, of course. If you'll let me get ready——'

'You said you were.'

'I'd like to comb my hair and put on some lipstick.'

'And you want me to leave while you do it?'

'Yes.'

Morgan took his sweater from the radiator. 'Right. Knock when you've finished.' He went towards his door. 'Oh. If you pack your things away we'll leave our luggage downstairs. I only brought an overnight case but we don't want to lug them round Paris all day, do we?'

'No.' She turned away from him and folded up her long skirt from the chair where she had left it. The jade pendant slid to the carpet and she picked it up. She remembered taking it off and putting it on the skirt.

'Do you want to wear that now?' he asked. 'It goes with the sweater.'

'Yes, I will.'

He held out his hand for it. She was about to tell him she could manage when she stopped. He would think she was frightened.

'Thank you.' She turned her back to him and lifted her hair up from her shoulders with her right hand. She felt his hands come round the front of her neck, and shivered inwardly, forcing herself to stand still even though every instinct was to break away. Then the touch of his fingers at the nape, a gentle butterfly touch that made the hairs tingle at the back of her neck until she felt breathless.

'Okay, done.'

'Thank you.'

She felt his hand on her hair and stiffened, tried to move away, but she couldn't *move*. Dear God, she thought, he's not going to try and kiss me, is he? Not after what he said——

'Don't let them take too much hair off, will you?' he said. 'It suits you like that.'

'N-no, of course not.' Heavens, she was stammering. What's the matter with me? she thought.

Then he was moving away. He said not another word, just walked out, and she was alone. She sat down on the bed and fingered the pendant. She was shaken, and yet it had been nothing. He had only wanted to comment on her hair, had only touched it lightly, casually.

She picked up her comb and combed her hair until her scalp tingled with the vigorous strokes. Then she found her lipstick and smoothed some on. A few minutes later, case packed and closed, she tapped on Morgan's door.

He had told her she was having her hair done; he hadn't mentioned that he had also asked them to give her a facial treatment, manicure, and full make-up.

Sara lay back as the last touches were made to her face by a skilled beautician who spoke very little English, but knew her job well, and waited to see what she looked like. The girl brushed surplus powder from her face, '*Et voilà, madame, c'est fini!*'

'*Merci.*' Sara sat up as the chair was raised, looked at herself in the mirror, closed her eyes in disbelief, then looked again. 'Good gracious,' she muttered. 'Is that really me?'

'*Pardon?*' The girl wrinkled her nose, puzzled, and Sara obligingly translated. The girl laughed.

'*Ah oui, c'est vous. Madame est très belle.*'

They had whipped her from one part of the salon to this place before, after she had had her hair cut and shaped, and she hadn't really had the opportunity to see herself. They hadn't taken a lot off, because she had asked them not to, but they had worked wonders. Her rich chestnut hair had been subtly cut to enhance the natural wave, and it fell softly round her face, curving to her neck and glowing rich and shiny. The face that looked back at her—the one she hadn't been sure was hers—was transformed with subtle make-up and eyeshadow and deft eyebrow shaping. She looked, and felt, totally different.

'*Merci,*' she said. She looked round the busy salon. There was no sign of Morgan. The beautician handed her a small white briefcase, and Sara shook her head.

'That's not mine,' she said in French, and the girl laughed, then explained that the *monsieur* had asked for her to have a complete make-up kit to suit her. She opened it. Inside were jars, bottles and eye-shadows and four lipsticks. Wow! thought Sara. She had never possessed more than one lipstick at a time in her life. She never wore any other kind of make-up either, and probably wouldn't after today, but it was fun to have.

The girl told her that monsieur was waiting for her in reception, and she would take her there. The pink overall that had covered her for the previous two hours was whipped away, and she walked steadily down the curving staircase to where Morgan was sitting waiting. He looked up, and for a moment it was as if he looked at a stranger, then he smiled and stood up and walked towards them. He thanked the girl, a note changed hands discreetly, and they were on their way out a few moments later.

Outside, in the hot afternoon sun, Sara turned to him. 'Well?' she said.

'You look stunning. Your hair's perfect.'

'Thank you. Now where?'

'Clothes.' He raised his arm, and a taxi slowed and stopped by them. She wondered if he ever had trouble getting one. Probably not. He was the kind of man who had only to whistle and everyone came running.

As they sat in it, she observed: 'You're like Svengali, aren't you?'

'Why?' He regarded her coolly.

'Taking me over. Make-up—clothes—the transformation.'

'Then I must remember to call you Trilby.' But he wasn't smiling, and she turned away. She shouldn't have said it; she didn't know why she had. She wondered if he would choose the clothes for her. Probably. What did it matter? It was only for a short time anyway. It was only a game to him. So why don't I look at it the same? she thought. Elizabeth would give her eye teeth to be where I am now. She sat up and looked around at the bustle of Paris. I'm here, she thought—enjoy it. He's doing this partly because of his father, and because mine asked him for help, and I should be grateful. But she felt as if she were being manipulated, like a marionette, and the word he had said kept coming back to her. Trilby. She should never have said that to him.

It was evening, and as they waited at the airport for their plane they drank coffee in the lounge. Sara looked at the people passing, and saw the glances that lingered on both her and Morgan, and smiled to herself. The transformation was complete. Cinderella's fairy godmother had waved her magic wand and told her she should go to the ball, and now she waited for the coach—only it had wings, not wheels, and it wouldn't vanish at midnight, it would continue afterwards.

She had two suitcases now, and the second was crammed with new clothes, and more to follow by post. And on her engagement finger she wore a large diamond on a gold band, and on her wrist, a diamond-studded Tissot watch.

She was wearing a dress of soft grey cashmere that had cost a fortune, gossamer-fine tights and plain black court shoes. She had never known what it was to be elegant before. Now she did, and she liked the feeling. But she was still herself inside, and perhaps Morgan didn't know that. Perhaps he thought the change went deeper than the surface. He looked at her appraisingly now, as if to see.

'Nervous?' he asked.

'No. Should I be?' She gave him a cool glance.

'No. You look very different.'

'You made sure of that. You've spent a small fortune on creating a fiancée who looks genuine. But it's *me* inside—I just want you to remember that.'

'I won't forget.' He stubbed out a cheroot in the ashtray. 'How can I?'

'What do you mean?'

'What I said. There's been a battle going on all day, ever

since we left the hotel this morning. You're prickly, on your guard——'

'Don't be absurd!' she snapped, and glared at him.

'Look at you now! Hackles raised, ready to fight. Relax, Sara, nobody's fighting you. I'm not. You're doing me a favour, remember?'

'How can *I* forget?' she said drily.

'Just so long as you don't when we get there. Louise will be alert to every gesture, every word on your part——'

'She'll think I adore you.' She smiled as she said it.

'That's the general idea. That's what I want her to think.'

'And that you adore me as well?'

'Of course.'

'And you can manage that?' She gave him a sweet little smile.

'I can. Want me to start now?' His eyes held a dark challenge, and she felt a tiny tremor of apprehension. Dear Lord, what a game it was!

'No. Time enough when we—get there.'

She saw the mockery at his mouth, heard it as he answered: 'Scared?'

'Of you—adoring me in public? Should I be?' She laughed, reached forward, and took hold of his hand. 'See —darling?'

'Mmm.' Morgan bent forward and kissed her fingers, and his eyes held the mockery now as he looked at her over her hand, and she resisted the instinctive impulse to pull herself away—and he knew. She deliberately relaxed, turned her smile to one of coquetry, and murmured:

'Oh, darling, dearest one, how your touch thrills me!'

He let go of her hand. 'Don't overdo it,' he said softly, and the mockery had gone from his face. 'Dear me, don't overdo it.'

Sara put her hand on the table. 'Perhaps we should have a rehearsal.'

'There's no time, they'll be calling the plane in a minute. Finish your coffee and we'll start walking.'

'Yes, dear.' She drank, put down her cup. 'I'm ready.'

He took her arm as they walked through the crowded concourse towards their gate. She caught a glimpse of their reflection in a glass door, and it was like watching two strangers, two tall handsome elegant strangers, a perfect couple walking towards their plane. She saw heads turn as they passed, both men and women watched them, and she knew why. Morgan was clever, and he knew what he was doing, and she wondered why she should hate him, suddenly, why she should want to hit, and run, and tell him to go alone—and she wondered why she was frightened of him, and of his power, and it seemed to her that if they had never gone to Georges' night club, and the incident in the doorway hadn't happened, then it might have all been different. But they had, and it had, and however much she tried to forget—and she was sure he had—she couldn't. The memory of his eyes, the look in them, and his words as he had asked her if she knew what she was doing, remained with her. It was why she was afraid, and hated him.

His grip tightened on her arm, as if he read her thoughts, and he said, very softly : 'Smile, darling.'

She tensed. It was like an order. 'Why?'

'Because I've just seen a near neighbour of mine.' He stopped, turned to her, looked down into her eyes, and gave her a look of complete love, so genuine that she felt herself reel under the impact. Sara caught her breath, then recovering fast, gazed back adoringly at him.

'Will that do?' she whispered, under cover of a radiant smile.

'Absolutely.' He laughed as if she had just said something of dazzling wit, and kissed her lightly, then walked on with her.

In the plane, she turned to him. 'Where's your "neighbour"?' she asked.

'Oh, at the back. He saw. He's a big-mouth too. It'll be all over Cannes tomorrow—and your description will be on everyone's lips.'

'That's nice,' she said with irony. 'Can I go home now?'

'Ha, ha. Witty as well as beautiful. It's going to be fun, being engaged to you—Trilby.'

'I wish I could say the same,' she retorted.

'I told you, look on it as a holiday.'

'But it won't be quite that, will it?' she murmured.

'It could be.' He seemed about to add something when the stewardess bent over them and asked if there was anything they wanted. It hadn't taken Sara long to realise that Morgan was known at the airport. Smiles and greetings from various members of staff followed them. Perhaps he flew often to and from Paris. The stewardess's eyes flickered briefly but comprehensively over Sara, and she smiled, but the smile was a cool professional one, the warmth was for him. She thought, dazedly, this is the effect he must have on people wherever he goes, and it explained, in part, why he had chosen her, on impulse, a perfect stranger to his part of the world, for the pretend engagement. He was not a man who could go through life unnoticed. So to produce a fiancée from England, from out of the blue, seemed the sort of thing he would do. He could have been meeting her secretly for some time....

'How old are you?' she asked abruptly, after the stewardess had left them, promising to bring champagne as soon as they were airborne.

'Thirty-three.' He looked at her and frowned. 'Why?'

'You know my age—it's rather odd if I don't know my fiancé's isn't it? You're nearly fourteen years older than me. Won't you be accused of cradle-snatching?'

He laughed. 'No. Fourteen years is nothing.'

'And how long are we supposed to have known each other?'

'Good question.' The seat-belt notice came on, and he

busied himself fastening his, then helped Sara to do hers. 'Say—two years?'

'All right. Which means you knew me just before I was eighteen.'

'That's about it. And I've loved you secretly since then— only of course, I had to be sure about you, being so young, so we've kept in touch, met in England, and now you've agreed to marry me. Right?'

She nodded. 'How did we meet?'

'I think we can adjust the time scale there slightly—just imply that it was because of our two fathers—no need for untruths there, everyone will accept that. They knew my father well on the Riviera. He never talked about the war— except to me—but he was known as a hero.'

Sara felt her eyes sting with sudden tears. She wished that Philip Bourne and Red Haldane had managed to meet, after the war. Her father would have loved that. She saw again in her mind's eye the drawing of Red that Morgan had produced at her uncle's house. He must have treasured it all these years. They had both been so young in those war days. Two young men, from different backgrounds, fighting together against a common enemy. And years later, in this strange way, being linked again with son and daughter.

She blinked a few times. 'I see.' Her voice was quiet. The roar of engines filled the plane, then movement, and they were taxiing down the runway. Soon, she thought, we'll be in the South of France. I'll be staying in the same house as Morgan for several weeks. Eating with him, going out with him, and everyone will envy me—but they won't know the truth. And when it's all over I suppose I'll have memories to take back with me to England, and I'll remember him, above all, because he's not a man anyone could forget easily. She turned to look out of the porthole; the ground was a blur now, moving away fast—and then down, down, as they lifted and soared into the night sky. She put her head back on the seat rest and closed her eyes. She felt empty inside, and it wasn't hunger, it was an ache in her heart, a sadness.

A car was waiting for them at Nice airport, a chauffeur-driven Jaguar, and Sara fell asleep as soon as it started. When she woke up, she was in a strange bed in a strange room, and it was early morning.

Sara sat up in bed. She was dressed only in her underclothes. Her dress was laid over a chair, her shoes by the side of it. She hadn't remembered arriving or undressing, so someone had done it for her. She wondered if it was Morgan. There were no sounds from anywhere; she was in a silent house in a silent world. Sara got out of bed and went over to the window and pulled back the soft velvet curtains, then stood there for a moment not believing what she saw.

She was on the ground floor, and outside her window, which was arched, and full length to the floor, was a stone-flagged terrace and a swimming pool. All were enclosed in a white-walled area, the walls of rough stone, smothered in ivy and climbing roses, and at the right end of it were two archways through which she caught a glimpse of a garden. The pool was filled with blue water and the whole effect was of stunning simplicity—and beauty. Sara opened her window and stepped out on to the terrace, and saw then that the wall outside her bedroom was covered with vines, the thick gnarled stems reaching up, fanning out from the ground, spreading out along the wall in a glory of green and purple. She reached up and picked a fat purple grape and ate it. Then she looked at the water, knelt down and put her hand in. It was cool and soft to her skin. Without even thinking about what she was doing, she took off her slip, flung it over a wrought iron chair, and slid into the water. The sky was a pearly grey, slightly misty, and she swam lazily on her back watching it. There wasn't a cloud to be seen. It was so utterly peaceful, just floating at a leisurely pace, kicking out occasionally to propel herself along, reaching the end and turning. . . .

'Good morning,' she heard his voice as she heard a window opening—the window next to hers—and Morgan stood there clad only in black pyjama trousers. Hard and muscular, arms akimbo, he stood and looked at her and she dived under and went to the side nearest him.

'I couldn't resist it,' she said. 'I hope you don't mind.'

'Mind? Why should I? Hang on, I'll join you.' He vanished, and Sara looked down at herself. The bra she wore was of black nylon and quite respectable, if rather lacy for swimming in. Her pants were the same, brief but adequate. And she wasn't his type anyway—although only they knew it. She swam a length underwater and when she surfaced he was in the pool with her. He swam towards her and stood beside her, looking down, amused, at her attire. 'I thought you'd like this, that's why I put you in the room next to mine. I often take a dip first thing before breakfast—although I don't usually bother with swimming trunks.'

'Oh!' She looked away hastily and he laughed.

'It's all right, I've got them on today.'

'Where's your housekeeper?' she asked.

'Probably in Cannes at the market. She goes first thing to be sure of decent fruit and vegetables.'

'Ah. Is there—er—anyone else here?'

'No. Only us.' He looked at her again, amused. 'Worried?' he asked softly.

'No. Who put me to bed?'

'I did. Don't look so alarmed. Martine was in bed when we arrived. She's up early, as you'll have gathered. I merely helped you off with your dress and popped you into bed— and you barely murmured. You were out like a light.'

'Oh. Thank you anyway.' She was very conscious of him, big and dark and unshaven, beside her. He was not comfortable to be near. He was too male—she moved away, casually, perhaps not casually enough, for Morgan followed her and caught hold of her, and she turned and struggled briefly. 'What are you——'

He was holding her left hand. 'Just checking if you'd kept your ring off. You don't want to lose it.' She looked at her bare hand. 'I took it off last night,' he added. 'It's on your bedside table with your watch.'

'You did a lot of looking after me last night,' she said. She was uneasy.

'Mmm, I did. Want to see around—if you've had enough time in the water?'

'Yes, please. It looks beautiful, the bit I've seen so far.'

'It is. I like it here—very much.' Morgan pulled himself out and reached down for her hand. He lifted her out as though she were a child, walked in through her window and said: 'I'll show you your bathroom. You've your own shower and toilet. Here,' he reached in and threw a large fluffy pink towel to her, 'get drying yourself. Want any help?'

'No, thanks.' She gave him a cool look. 'I can manage.'

He grinned. 'I thought you'd say that.' He went into the bathroom and came out with a second, smaller towel. 'Mind if I borrow this? I'll give you another one,' and he began drying himself before she could answer. It seemed too cosy and intimate to Sara, who walked away from him and went to the open window. She wasn't going to take anything off with him there. Did he think she was? What the hell's he playing at? she thought, disturbed and faintly annoyed.

'I want to talk to you, Sara.'

'All right. But let me get dressed first, will you?'

'That's what I want to talk to you about. Louise and Jack will be coming over later. Will you wear the pants outfit we bought yesterday?'

'The blue one?' She looked round the large room. 'I don't know where my case is.'

'In here.' He slid back a mirrored door in the white wall,

and her new clothes were hanging neatly on the rail. 'I unpacked them for you.'

'Quite the valet, aren't you?' She was vaguely annoyed. 'I suppose you put my undies away as well?'

'No. They're in your case.' Morgan delved into the recesses of the fitted wardrobe and produced it.

'All right, I can choose *those* myself,' she said crossly, and he looked at her and smiled slightly.

'I thought it was going to be all sweetness and light—darling,' he said, and the laughter was only just concealed.

'When we've got company to impress, yes,' she retorted. 'But we're alone, aren't we?'

'Indeed we are.' He walked over to where she stood, towel casually slung over her shoulders. It was a very large towel. He touched her shoulders, resting his hands lightly on them. 'Quite alone. You said, last night at the airport, that we ought to have a rehearsal. What better time than now? While we're—alone.'

Sara stood very still. 'It might not be such a good idea,' she said. Her heart hammered in her breast. What was in his mind? Dear God, she felt almost dizzy at the thought of him making love to her. But she was sober, stone cold sober, and this wasn't a dimly lit doorway in Paris, this was a bedroom, and she wasn't going to fling herself at him ever again——

Morgan traced a line down her cheek with his finger. 'You're quite safe,' he said. 'Quite—safe,' and he bent his head and kissed her on the mouth, a very respectable old-fashioned kiss. 'See?'

She stood there, unable to move, eyes wide. 'Is that it? The—rehearsal?' she said, controlling her voice with difficulty.

'No.' He took hold of her hand and lifted it to his mouth and kissed the cupped palm very gently. 'This is also something I shall do—like—this,' and he did it again. His lips were warm, his breath sweet and equally warm, and she wanted to pull her hand away, but didn't.

'That's lesson number two,' she murmured, as if it were all a game—which, of course, it was. 'I'll remember that. C-can I get my clothes on now?'

'No.' He removed the towel from her shoulders and flung it on the bed, then let his eyes caress her entire body. She was trying to steady her breathing, but it was difficult. His eyes were on her breasts as if he couldn't look away and she felt as if he could see her heart bumping violently.

'Stop looking at me,' she muttered. 'Please——' She raised her hands to her breasts to cover them and he looked at her, right into her eyes, his dark and shadowed.

'You have the most incredible figure,' he murmured. 'Simply beautiful.'

'But it's not for sale, remember? It's not part of the—agreement.'

'No—true. But a man can look. I'm seeing no more than if you were in a bikini—and I want to let you see that I'm perfectly controlled, so that you'll be reassured, Sara.'

'You could have fooled me,' she answered, and turned away to pick up the towel. Her hand was shaking and she dropped it, and he bent, scooped it up, and wrapped it round her tightly.

'There now. Satisfied?' he teased.

'I will be when you go.' Morgan laughed and pulled her to him.

'Relax. The lesson's nearly over.'

'Nearly?' she squeaked, held tightly, unable to move. 'What do you——' Her next word was lost as he showed her what he meant. He enfolded her tightly in his arms, and began to kiss her.

CHAPTER FIVE

'WHY—why—are you doing this?' she demanded breath-lessly. She had managed to struggle free—although it was quite obvious to her that had he not wanted to release her, she would have been still helplessly imprisoned.

'I told you, it's a rehearsal. Relax, Sara, just relax and enjoy it. You're in a different world now, a brittle, feather-light world of easy emotions and passing fancies. People are shallow and fickle here—and never, never serious. You must remember that.' He stroked her cheek gently and laughed. 'To kiss, to be kissed, is nothing,' he added softly.

'But I'm not like that!'

'You take life too seriously,' he told her.

'No!' she burst out. 'I don't. Is this your choice? Your world? Do you like it like this?' Her eyes blazed with a mixture of anger and the excitement he had roused in her.

'I live here by choice.'

'That doesn't answer my question!' She stamped her foot in sheer frustration. 'Answer me!'

'No. I'm neither shallow nor brittle—but I act the part, because I choose to. I have my reasons, Sara.'

'And what are they?' She lifted her chin defiantly and heard him draw in his breath sharply.

'One day I may tell you.'

'Hah! That's no answer at all.' She stood, arms akimbo, hands on hips, and stared at him. She was not aware of the picture she made. She saw only the spark and something lit deep within his eyes as she stood there defiantly and chal-lenged him with her very being. Then he stepped back, and it seemed as if the shutters came down. His expression changed, and he turned away.

'You'd better get dressed,' he said, picking up the towel he had dropped. His voice was like that of a stranger. Oh no, you don't, Sara thought. You don't start something and then, when it gets awkward for you, end it.

She followed him and took hold of his arm. She felt the power of him, but she was no longer afraid of him; she was too angry for that.

'Look at me,' she demanded, and he turned back to her, his eyes narrowed, his mouth taut. 'I'm here because *you* persuaded me to come — and I'm damned if we're going to talk just when *you* want to!'

'You've a fine temper on you,' he said softly. 'And you're very determined. But no woman tells me what to do — you'd do well to remember that, Sara.'

'And you'd do well to remember that I'm a *person*, not a chattel!' she stormed. Her cheeks burned, and her bosom heaved with anger. 'Damn you, Morgan Haldane, you've not bought *me*, even if you have bought fancy clothes and jewellery. You'll never buy me, do you hear me? *Never!*'

'Oh, I hear you very well. You make yourself quite clear,' he said quietly, dangerously. 'Be thankful you're a woman, Sara. I don't allow anyone to speak to me as you have done, any——'

She slapped him hard and satisfyingly across his face, whirled away and picked up her towel, as though to defend herself. He stood there, looked steadily at her, then turned and walked out through the open window.

Sara sat down, trembling, on the bed, biting her lip. The look Morgan gave her spoke more than words ever could. There had been explosive force, tautly controlled, in that look. There had been more. For an instant she had glimpsed a trace of his forebears, had seen an American Indian warrior — she had seem something of that in the sketch of his father, but just now, in Morgan, it had been very pronounced. And it seemed to Sara that she knew what it would be like to have him as an enemy. She didn't want

to be his enemy; she didn't want him to hate her. It had to
be done, and it was better done now, before she had too
much time to think about it, and be frightened of the con-
sequences. She walked out on to the terrace and paused
outside his window, then knocked, keeping her eyes averted
in case he was dressing.

'Morgan?'

'Yes?' He appeared from the shadowy room. He wore
black jeans, nothing else.

'I'm very sorry for losing my temper.'

He was towelling his hair dry. He looked at her for a
moment, and the deep, terrifying anger she had seen had
gone. 'Then we'll forget it. I think Martine has returned—
I heard a car. How long will you be?'

'I'll be ready and dressed in five minutes.' She hesitated
in case he wanted to add anything, and when he said nothing, she went on: 'I—won't let you down.'

'I know you won't.' He nodded and turned away. 'I'll
knock on your door in five minutes, then I'll show you
round.'

She was effectively dismissed. Thoughtfully, still shaken,
she went back into her room. The deep-pile white carpet
was damp in parts from their wet feet. She avoided tread-
ing on the patches, went over to her case, and opened it to
look for her new underwear.

Within five minutes she was ready, and took a last look
in the long wardrobe mirror as she waited. She wore the
outfit Morgan had suggested, one they had bought in Paris
the previous day, and she regarded her reflection with some
surprise at the transformation wrought by couture clothes.
It was simple and elegant and comfortable, slim-fitting
trousers and matching blouson in a light blue glazed cotton. The blouson top hugged her slender waist, and the
sleeves came just below her elbows. The open collar
finished in a deep V, that was low enough but not indis-
creetly so, and the overall effect was stunning. Her hair, still

damp, framed her face, curling slightly at the ends as it always did before it was dry. She had put on one of the new lipsticks, smoothed in the merest whisper of blusher, and touched in her eyebrows with the soft crayon-like pencil in the beauty kit. 'You'll do,' she said, just as the tap came at the door. She put on her ring and went to open it.

'I'm ready,' she said.

Morgan nodded. 'Then I'll show you round, and afterwards we'll breakfast on the front terrace.' He gave her a brief, all-encompassing glance, then indicated that she should walk to the right. The hallway was wide, with a shiny tiled floor in muted greys. Light slanted in from the room ahead and as she went in, she gasped, looked, turned and said: 'It's gorgeous!'

'Thank you. This is the summer dining room. We eat here in the evenings—and this is where I serve the buffet when I give parties.' She gazed round the spacious room, with its two elegant french windows open on to a terrace with low walls beyond which glinted the sea. The room itself had a wrought iron staircase leading off at the far end, and beside it, glass doors open to another room. A large glass-topped table had fine green leather seats with wrought iron legs set around it. Along the outer walls, between the windows, were several easy chairs. The walls were pale pearl grey, and large ferny plants stood on intervals on tall stands.

Morgan walked across to the open windows and stepped outside. Tall cypress trees stirred in a faint breeze, and the air was scented with the flowers the grew atop the low wall. A wrought iron table and two chairs were outside, the chairs facing the sea. Sara followed him. 'This is where we'll breakfast,' he said. 'And now, come and see the library.'

She was looking upwards at the rooms over the ground floor. Ten arched windows faced the sea. 'How many bedrooms are there?' she asked, in wonder.

'Seven—and seven bathrooms. My father built this place a few years after the war.'

It had been built with love, you could see that. Each room was a revelation, a polished gem—the library, morning room, study, and the bedrooms. Morgan was clearly a wealthy man, as, equally obviously, had his father been before him. And Sara sensed something else, something Morgan wasn't telling—and she couldn't ask, because she didn't even know what the question was. Morgan was the polite host, cool, caring—yet impersonal. He took her finally to the kitchen, where Martine was preparing vegetables. A small thin woman, with grey hair severely scraped back in a bun, and button-black eyes, she regarded Sara shrewdly before coming forward to shake hands on Morgan's introduction. For the first time, Sara heard him say in French:

'Mademoiselle Sara *est ma fiancée*, Martine.'

To say that Martine was surprised would have been putting it mildly—but she hid it well. '*Enchanté, mademoiselle*,' she murmured. '*Bienvenue au Villa Esterel.*'

'*Merci bien, madame.*'

The little woman's eyes lit up. '*Vous parlez français, mademoiselle?*' she exclaimed.

It was now or never. Sara had a flash of intuition which told her that the relationship between the housekeeper and herself could get off on a good footing right away if she spoke fluent French. Praying inwardly, and very briefly, that her accent wouldn't let her down, she answered, in French:

'Alas, only a little, but I am learning, *madame*.' She saw by the glint of laughter in the French woman's eyes that she had done well enough, for now.

'But your accent is impeccable, *mademoiselle*!' the housekeeper said also in French.

'Thank you,' Sara smiled. Morgan had stood aside during their little exchange, silent but watchful. Sara sensed his eyes on them both. The deception had begun, and suddenly she was filled with a calm strength.

She picked up a courgette from the chopping board on the table. In French she went on to the housekeeper: '*Madame*, I'd appreciate it if you'd show me *your* way of cooking these some time. I am, alas, not such a good cook as I would like to be——'

'Ah!' She'd done it. A sense of rightness flooded her at the delight on Martine's face. 'With pleasure, *mademoiselle*. I shall be delighted, any time you wish. You are interested in cooking?'

'Very,' admitted Sara, 'but only simple English food, you understand? Mr Haldane has told me you are the best cook on the Riviera—if I could learn a little from you, I'd be very pleased.' She spoke with growing confidence, only a slight hesitation before certain words, but memory of school lessons returned quickly, and she and her father had often had conversations in French just for fun. They were paying off now.

'Any time, *mademoiselle*,' Martine assured her. 'And now, the breakfast is awaiting you both when you are ready for it.'

'Right away, Martine,' Morgan spoke for the first time since introducing them. There was a look of something that could be amusement in his eyes. 'On the terrace, if you will.'

'Assuredly, *monsieur*. The coffee is ready.'

'Come on, Sara,' Morgan indicated the open door leading outside. 'We'll walk round by the gardens.'

Outside he said to her, 'Clever—very clever.'

Sara hid a smile. 'Martine, you mean? I *am* interested in cooking—and you did say she was good.'

'She is. It isn't quite what I meant.' He paused by a low wall that led along the broad terrace, and looked out to sea, as if drinking in the view. 'You got her on your side right away. I didn't tell you before, but Martine's a good friend of the housekeeper at Louise and Jack's.' He laughed. 'The news won't be long getting there. The grapevine round here is far more efficient than the French telephone service.'

'Er—does Martine like Louise?' she asked.

'Not particularly. Louise is one of those women who wouldn't bother to learn French, on the principle that the peasants should take the trouble to learn English.'

'Charming,' Sara commented.

'Precisely. No doubt a glowing account of my fiancée will be forwarded to Madame Roche and filtered through to all the staff at Louise's before the day's out.'

'And no doubt,' Sara said softly, 'Louise will be made aware of it.'

'I shouldn't be surprised. The French are very subtle— and Louise isn't the most popular employer round here. They like Jack, but then it's difficult not to. But her——' he shrugged. 'One gets—impressions.'

'She sounds a bundle of laughs,' she observed.

They stood near the table and watched Martine deftly setting their places. 'A bundle of laughs is precisely what she's not. Louise is totally lacking in any sense of humour. There's only one thing important to her—and that's herself.'

'I can't wait to meet her,' said Sara, voice heavy with sarcasm. She looked at him as they walked towards the ready table. 'I'm beginning to understand your reasons for this charade, more and more, with everything I hear.'

'Just remember, you've started off well.'

'You could have warned me about Martine.'

'Knowing Louise's housekeeper? It might have inhibited you. As it was you did and said just the right things.'

'Thank you.' This as he passed her the plate of flaky hot croissants. She looked directly into his eyes. 'Why?' she asked.

'Why what?'

'I think you know.' A sense of something not quite right

had been growing steadily within her. She was always sensitive to atmosphere, and there was the growing conviction in her that he had other, subtler, far more secret reasons for his asking her than those he had given. And she felt a shimmer of tension, sudden and startling, reach out and touch her. On the surface, nothing wrong. Two people sitting at a table outside a beautiful home, eating breakfast—beneath the surface, swirling undercurrents——

'No. Tell me.' Morgan had gone very still. He paused in the act of buttering his croissant, put down his knife, and looked at her. His eyes were almost mesmeric in their hardness—and she couldn't look away. It had suddenly gone on a deeper level than a mere conversation; it was in a way now, more puzzling and strange than anything else that had happened.

She shivered, icy cold touching her shoulder blades. How powerful he was she had only surmised before, now the hard strength, the depth of his character, were only too evident. He was a deeply disturbing man, and she was not immune from that power to disturb. 'I don't think you've been completely honest with me,' she said.

'You mean I've lied to you?'

'No, not exactly. I just think—you've only told me half the story of why you want me here.'

'And why do you think that?' His eyes never left her face. She felt as if she were drowning in their depths. She had to break the spell somehow. She picked up the coffee pot and poured two cups. Her hand wasn't quite steady, and the silver spout of the coffee pot touched the china cup and clinked sharply.

'Black or white?' she asked.

'White. Why do you think that?' he repeated. Sara concentrated for a moment on pouring in the hot milk, careful now not to touch the cup. Then she drank some. She needed it. But now, strangely, she wasn't frightened. She was a fighter, and something deep inside her told her she wasn't mistaken, and this gave her the strength she needed.

'Because of the kind of man you are. I've seen you in action——' she swallowed, 'and I'm damned sure you wouldn't let a woman like Louise scare you—you're not frightened of anything or anybody. I may be only a country bumpkin, but I'm not stupid, Morgan. Nor are you. You've given me reasons for this engagement— and I accepted them, odd though the set-up seemed. But I didn't know you then. That was in England. I've been with you, travelled with you, seen Paris with you, since then, and I've seen the way you have of dealing with people—the drunken American, Georges, the staff at the fashion house and jeweller's—at the airport—and it doesn't add up.' She paused to marshall her thoughts and gather breath, and he said very quietly:

'Don't stop there, Sara. Please continue. You intrigue me.'

'Do I?' She bit into the flaky croissant, belatedly realising that she was extremely hungry. 'At least you're not telling me I'm mad.'

'I wouldn't do that.'

'You would if you felt like it,' she retorted. 'And that's part of my argument. You'd say exactly what you wanted to say to *anyone*. And that includes Louise. And because, so far, you haven't told me I'm crazy, it means to me that I'm on the right track, doesn't it?'

Morgan smiled, but it wasn't his usual smile. It was a thin smile, and his eyes were narrowed, and his face was like a carved mask, and she froze momentarily. Damn him! 'Perhaps,' he said softly. The word sent a shiver down her spine. She felt almost dizzy, as if his power could make her weak—yet it made her more determined. She'd never met a man like him before—she didn't imagine there were too many like him in the world—but she was her father's daughter, and she possessed his courage, and if Morgan thought he could intimidate her he was in for a shock.

'Then why don't you tell me?' she demanded. 'The *real* reason I'm here. And don't give me the old guff implying you're scared of Louise! Hah!' she laughed derisively. 'Because I'll fall off my chair laughing if you do.'

She thought for a moment that she had gone too far. For just one second she thought he would explode. The moment passed, then he took a deep breath. 'You're quite right,' he said. His voice was soft. He looked at his watch. 'Finish eating,' he went on. 'I'm going to take you somewhere.'

'To do with—what I've been asking?'

'Yes.'

'You're going to take me now?'

'You want to know, don't you?'

'Why don't you just tell me?' She was beginning to wish that she hadn't delved too deeply. Where was he going to take her, for heaven's sake? What place could he show her that would explain this feeling she'd had for a while that something was awry?

'No. You'll understand why when we're there. Finish your croissants.'

'I don't want any more. Morgan?'

'Yes?' She didn't like the expression on his face. She would rather he was angry, shouting—anything except that dark implacable look. That was the word to describe him— implacable. Why hadn't she just left it?

'I don't—want to know.'

'But you're going to.' He stood up. 'If you've finished eating we'll leave. Martine won't be very pleased. You've only had one croissant.'

'Oh, all right.' She put apricot jam on a second one, bit it, and stared at him. 'Satisfied now?'

The side of his mouth quirked. 'Yes. Come on, this way.'

There were steps down at the far end of the terrace, into a sunken garden, full of flowering shrubs and trees, and the air had a soft sweet scent to it. At the far end, a wrought iron gate was set in a stone archway, Morgan opened the gate, and two cars were parked, facing a driveway. One was a Mercedes, the other a maroon Jaguar. He opened the passenger door on the Jaguar and Sara slid in. The seat was hot with the concentrated sun pouring in, and she moved uneasily. Morgan switched on the engine, and cool air blew in. He drove along, the drive curving down towards the road, and she looked back to see the villa high above them. No wonder there was such a view, she thought, dazed.

Her mind raced on, exploring possibilities. Where on earth could Morgan be going? She knew he wouldn't tell her even if she asked, but she felt uneasy. She thought she knew him—but he was still a stranger.

'I—thought Louise would be coming over,' she said.

'Later. We'll only be an hour.' She digested that crumb of information in silence. They weren't going far. Cannes? Nice? To his hotel—or one of the restaurants he ran with Jack? To see someone? She looked at him as he drove. They were on the coast road winding by the sea now, and he drove fast; nothing overtook them, and the road was a passing blur. Only the sea remained steady in the distance, sparkling in the sun, a deep blue blending with the sky.

Then came a side road and Morgan roared up it, a steep climb, and she held on to the seat praying he would slow down, but he said: 'Relax. I know where I'm going.'

'Which is more than I do,' she retorted, and he laughed.

'You soon will. Very soon.'

They drove through a small village, only one street, with old ladies sitting in doorways knitting, and a couple of dogs scratching themselves on the dusty pavement, and he had decreased speed until they were past it, and still climbing, up, up, into the hills. The trees were luxurious and green, and the fields stretched away at either side of the road, which was narrow and getting narrower, and she began to relax. There was a calm sense of inevitability about the situation. Nothing she could do.

Then Morgan was slowing, and she saw, on the right, ahead of them, in a long stone wall, a pair of wrought iron gates, which were open. Inside was a notice: '5 Kms.' was all it said. They were at crawl speed now, going along a tree-sheltered drive that curved on and round to the left, and then a house came in sight—only it was more like a *château*, all grey stone, old and scarred and very dignified-looking. Morgan cruised to a stop by the entrance, switched off, and looked at her.

'You can get out now,' he said.

Sara looked at the building. 'Where are we?' she asked faintly.

'Get out and you'll see.' He opened his door, uncurled his lean length, got out and slammed the door shut. Then her door was opening, and Morgan stood looking down at her, looking amused. Not angry, not violent—but amused. 'Come on,' he said.

Sara got out and stood there, then she heard a door opening, looked, and saw a sight she was never to forget as long as she lived. A nun was walking down the steps, beaming all over her face, and spilling out with her came at least half a dozen small children, running to keep up with her, their tiny legs stumbling down the steps as they shouted excitedly. Sara, incapable of moving for the moment, stood rooted to the spot and watched Morgan go forward to shake hands with the nun. She was only tiny, and he towered over her. Two of the children were jumping up at him, clutching his arms, and he bent and scooped them up, then turned to Sara and said: 'Come and meet the family.'

It was a dream. She was still in bed. She had never got up that morning. This—*this* couldn't be real. Only it was. She walked forward and Morgan said: 'Sister Teresa, this is Sara Bourne, a friend from England.'

'How nice to meet you, my dear.' The little woman, as English as Sara herself, shook her hand. Her rosy-cheeked face was beaming with pleasure.

'Sara's come to see round. Is that convenient, Sister?'

'Of course, Mr Haldane. The older children are at their lessons now, but they'll be only too glad of an excuse to break for a few moments. What a pleasure it is to meet someone from England, Miss Bourne. Do come in, I'll tell Mother Superior you're here. Now children, behave. Do put Emile and Maria down, Mr Haldane. They're so pleased to see you they forget their manners, I'm afraid.' She took Sara's arm. 'This way, mind the steps. Oh, what a lovely surprise, isn't it, children?' The other four followed Sara, staring at her solemnly, as Morgan led the way in, followed by the little nun, who was practically running to keep up. They entered a wide hall which was bare of furniture and had white-painted walls, upon which light streamed in from a stained glass window at one side, making coloured patterns on the plain surface. There were doors leading off, and a long corridor, and a wide staircase. Distantly came children's voices raised in song, and from somewhere nearer a desk lid slammed shut, and a woman's voice, faint but distinct, said: 'Levez-vous.'

It was clearly a school of some kind; that much had registered in Sara's very confused mind. Sister Teresa, still chattering to Morgan—she had scarcely stopped for breath since opening the door—was disappearing down the corridor, following Morgan, still with his two passengers, and the tangle of children who ran ahead of Sara, giggling. They were dressed in identical blue outfits, a kind of mini boiler suit over white blouses. Yet they couldn't be more than three or four at most in age, surely too young for school.

A door opened. Sara heard a voice: 'Morgan, mon cher! Quelle surprise!' and he turned and beckoned her, and she went into a small room. Behind a desk sat a very motherly old woman in nun's habit. She was standing to come round the desk as Sara went in, and took the children from Morgan and put them firmly down on the floor. Then she saw

Sara, and smiled warmly. Morgan introduced them, and the Mother Superior spoke in good English, welcoming her, telling Sister Teresa to take the children back to their group, and then they were seated.

'I'd like to show Sara round, Mother Augustus,' Morgan said.

'But yes, of course!' She twinkled her eyes at Sara. She was much plumper than the little nun, but there was nevertheless a similarity of features, a calmness and serenity about both faces that Sara found pleasant to see. 'But first, you will take tea with me? Or a little wine, perhaps?' She chuckled. 'Home-made, of course—but you will like it, I think.' She pressed a bell on her desk.

'Wine would be very nice,' said Morgan. 'Sara?'

'Oh, yes, please.' She sat there trying to look intelligent, but feeling totally confused.

'Good, good. The dandelions are so plentiful, you know. And the children enjoy picking them for Sisters Maria and Hélène. We are quite a self-sufficient little community, as you will see, Miss Bourne. We grow all our own vegetables, and we have several dozen hens, and three goats.' She beamed at Sara, who smiled back as if she understood perfectly. But she didn't. She understood nothing at all, only that this was a place where Morgan was clearly respected and well known, and he had brought her here because she had been asking too many questions. Now she was wishing she hadn't, because there was no way that she could see any connection with her deception as Morgan's fiancée. He had introduced her only as a friend. That was another odd thing.

A young nun, scarcely older than Sara, knocked and came in, and was despatched for wine and biscuits, and she listened to Morgan and the nun speaking. He was asking if there were any problems, and the Mother Superior told him that there had been some trouble with the drains, and he told her he'd send someone to look at them.

The wine arrived, and it was delicious, sweet and light; there were home-made biscuits on a plate and Mother Augustus begged Morgan to smoke if he wished, and produced a large ashtray that said 'A present from Blackpool', while Sara wondered if she were going crazy.

Then, ceremonies over, wine drunk and biscuits eaten, they were on their way out. They went up the stairs and into a large dormitory full of bunk beds, and Mother Augustus turned to Sara as Morgan walked over to check a suspect window catch, and said quietly and with some emotion: 'Mr Haldane is such a wonderful man. He is never too busy to come if we need him, you know. Look, now, Miss Bourne—see, nothing is too much trouble.' She nodded in Morgan's direction. He was frowning, opening and closing the window, fiddling with the catch, concentrating.

Sara knew she would burst if she didn't find out something of why they were here soon. 'He—he's not told me anything, Mother Augustus,' she said. 'He just brought me here—and I'm delighted, of course, but is he—has he some connection with this school?' There, it was said.

'Why, bless you, my child,' the nun almost laughed in surprise. 'Mr Haldane is our *patron*! We are only here due to his kindness, and that of his late father. He owns this castle, and he pays for everything. It is a house for orphaned children and refugees, Miss Bourne.'

CHAPTER SIX

An orphanage, owned and run by Morgan. Sara gaped at the nun, who chuckled and patted her arm. 'Come,' she whispered. 'It seems he is busy.' She ushered the dazed Sara into the corridor. 'Did he not tell you?'

'No.' Sara shook her head.

'That is not surprising. No one knows of his connection with us, of course. He is a very private man, is he not? So like his dear father. Did you know him?' Sara shook her head. It seemed, for the moment, all she was doing.

'Ah, there, I see. Mr Haldane—his father—bought this *château* at the end of the war, when there were so many refugee children from all over Europe. Many would have died, I am sure, but for him. He had rescued some from the Germans, and that must have started the plan in his mind.

'There were so many homeless then, and orphaned in the war. I came here also in 1945, with some Dutch and French children, and I have been here ever since. We have had many hundreds pass through our hands in these past years, and grown up and married now—many that would not even have lived. And now it begins again. Only a few months ago we took twelve Vietnamese boat children. All are settled happily and learning French and English. When they are sixteen they will leave, of course, but by that time they will be equipped for a trade—Mr Haldane, as his father did before him, sees that tutors are brought in to teach the older ones useful work. Two are waiters in his hotel, and one girl a receptionist there—and many come back to see us from time to time, with their families,' She shook her head, and there were tears in her eyes. 'He was a saint, Miss Bourne, and his son is as good.'

'I didn't realise,' Sara said quietly.

'It was a surprise to see you. He has never brought any-one before—it is as if he doesn't wish the world to know of his kindness, and we accept his wish for secrecy. We want for nothing, ever.'

'I can see that.' Sara looked around at the airy corridor in which they stood. All was clean, the walls newly painted, the stone floor in good condition.

'He was born here. And when his mother died, when he was only a child, we brought him up, that is why he is like a son to me.' The nun raised her finger as they heard Morgan's footsteps across the dormitory floor. 'Ssh! Here he is.'

He came out dusting his hands. 'I've fixed it.' There was a smudge on his cheek, and he didn't look hard at all, he looked very—human, somehow. Sara looked at him with new eyes, and it was at that moment she knew she loved him.

'And now, the schoolrooms. There are of course, several more dormitories; we have fifty children altogether, at the moment, but I fear they all look alike—the dormitories, I mean,' and chuckling, she led them along the corridor. As they followed, Morgan looked at Sara.

'I gather she told you,' he said drily. 'I can see by your face that you've had some sort of a shock.'

'You could have warned me,' she whispered, still shaken.

He smiled. 'Oh no. You asked—I brought you. I would have told you going back anyway. Pity I didn't see your face.' He took her arm as they went down the stairs and into the hallway, and Sara trembled at his touch. It was like an electric shock along her arm. She was more devastated by her own new-found knowledge than by what the nun had told her, but she mustn't let him see that.

She watched as Mother Augustus opened a door, and there was a hushed silence, and a scraping of chairs as children rose to their feet. Taking a deep breath, Sara followed her in.

'So now you know. It's strictly between us, Sara. No one else, not even Martine, has any idea.' Morgan was driving back down the twisting road, and it was nearly lunchtime. The sun was high in the sky, glinting off the hood of the car, dazzling, and Sara sat listening to him. She was learning to accept the knowledge of the home, but she was still dazed with the knowledge that she was in love with him.

'It's marvellous. But what's it got to do with our "engagement"?' she asked.

He slowed the car, pulled in at the side, and switched off. 'I'll tell you. Listen carefully because it's quite complicated. Ready?'

She nodded. She wasn't. She didn't think she was ready for any more surprises, but she might as well get them all over with at once. 'Let's get out.' Morgan opened his door, and Sara opened hers and stood at the side of the road. She looked around her. If a herd of elephants blowing trumpets suddenly appeared, she wasn't going to show astonishment. She might faint, but she wouldn't look at all dismayed.

'Well?' she said.

Morgan took her hand and led her up into the field at the side of the road. Perhaps he's going to make love to me, she thought—and wondered why she didn't want to escape any more. 'Where are you taking me?' she asked, and it didn't matter, but it seemed polite to ask.

'Wait and see.' The field was rough, and the track they walked was narrow, and they had only just left the *château* so they weren't so far away, and might even see it. Perhaps he wanted to show it to her from a distance. Perhaps he might kiss her as well....

'Right—stop!' Sara looked round. They were in some trees, and that was all she could see.

'Right, I've stopped.' She looked at him. She ached to

have him touch her, and hold her, but she looked at him as though politely waiting for his next command.

'Now—look!' He turned her slightly round by the simple expedient of putting his hands on her upper arms and moving her, and she saw the clearing in the trees—and in the middle of the clearing, in the distance, a derelict watermill. The building was in two parts, separated only by the huge waterwheel, and plants and wild flowers grew in profusion from the walls, even from the guttering on the patched roof. It had a faded charm about it, even though it was clearly in poor condition.

'It's—interesting,' she murmured faintly.

'It's also Louise's—as is this strip of land. And I want it,' said Morgan.

It seemed as if a lot of pieces in a giant jigsaw suddenly fell into place. There were a great many more pieces missing—but a small portion of a large picture was emerging. Sara stood silently, and he took her hand and drew her forward towards it. As they neared it she saw just how large it was—and how much work needed doing. And it belonged to Louise—only Morgan wanted it. But what could Sara possibly have to do with *that* fact?

She shook her head slowly. 'Mmm,' she said. 'This is Louise's place, *you* want it—and that's why we've become engaged. Ha, ha—very simple really! I should have guessed before. Silly *me*!'

He caught her hand more tightly and pulled her to him. 'Got it in one try, little Miss Trilby.'

She shook herself free, irritated by his tone, by the Miss Trilby—by *him*. And she wished he wouldn't *touch* her. Didn't he know why?

'All right,' she said, 'you'd better tell me. It's obviously connected with the Home—because it's not a mile back down the road. But if, as you say, you presumably want to buy it from Louise, how is my being engaged to you going to help? If she's as you've described her reaction would be surely to tell you to get lost.'

'Mmm, sound reasoning—except that, one, she doesn't know I want it, and I've no intention of telling her, and two, she's been after Jack for a while to buy out my share in the restaurants—which may sound strange for a woman who's lusting after me, but Louise is greedy. She'd like Jack to be the sole owner—more kudos for her, and lots more money to be made by Jack. She doesn't like my business methods and thinks I'm holding him back.'

'And are you?'

'No.' He regarded her with amusement. 'She knows nothing about business. She has grandiose ideas—it's God help Jack when she gets control, as she will, but that's his problem, not mine.'

'I thought you liked him?' she queried.

'I do. He's so much money he wouldn't notice the difference. He's worth millions.'

'Are you?' she asked flippantly.

'Would it make any difference if I were?'

'Not a bit,' she shrugged.

'That's fine. It causes too much trouble as it is.'

'What does?'

'Money.'

'Yes. I suppose——' Sara thought of Uncle Herbert. His fortune could be numbered in thousands, but it hadn't brought him much happiness, not with a grasping wife and daughters. Although that might well have changed, since Morgan's visit. 'I must ring him,' she said, remembering.

'You've lost me.' Morgan didn't look lost, he didn't look anything, except slightly amused.

'We were talking about money, right?' He nodded. 'And it causing trouble——' He nodded again. 'And it made me think about my uncle—he's not wealthy by your standards, but he does have money, and it's not brought him happiness—and it reminded me that I ought to ring him, that's all.'

'Thank you for the explanation. I thought I might have missed some essential part of our conversation,' he said gravely.

'And it bothered you? Hah!'

'No, it didn't bother me at all.'

Sara glared at him. 'Look, are we here to look at this mill or not?'

'We've seen it, that's all. We can go now. Back home—and if you can,' he seemed to be hesitating, 'find your way, when you meet Louise, to mention the restaurants, in a kind of manner to imply how happy you are I'm in partnership with Jack——'

'She'll want even more to get out?' she interjected sharply.

'You hit the nail on the head every time.'

'Don't give me the old flannel,' she snapped back. 'You want me to do it—okay, I will. But tell me this. *Why* do you want this land, and this mill?'

'I want to expand the home. This is the only way to go. The mill, restored, would be ideal for a community for the older ones, preparing them for the big world. Only a step away, but a different atmosphere. I've thought about it for a while, but there was the insurmountable obstacle of Louise.'

'And then you met me,' she said drily.

'Yes.'

'I'll do it. If you think it'll work.'

'It will. I know Louise, I know the way *her* mind works. Come on, let's go.'

They set off walking back towards the car. 'But,' said Sara, after some thought, '*how*——'

'How does it get me the property? She'll be mad at *you* being engaged to me. When I hint to Jack I'd consider him buying me out—and add casually that if he flung this bit of land in it'd be a deal, she'll bite.'

'Have you ever made any mistakes in business?' she asked sarcastically

'Yes. When I was younger—and learning. Not recently.'

'Is it so important to you? This expansion, I mean?'

'Yes. The house was a big thing to my father, therefore it is to me.'

'How come the coincidence of Louise having the land right next to yours?'

'Simple. At the end of the war when my father bought the *château*, he had a business partner—Louise's father. They bought adjoining pieces of land, for eventual development. Then her father died, leaving it to his wife. It passed to Louise eventually, but it means nothing to her. She's never done anything with it.'

'Her father was English?'

'Yes.'

'Was he wealthy too?' she asked.

'He was. He gambled his money away—as she does now.'

'Oh, no!'

'Oh, yes. Jack is forever signing the bill for some casino or other. She's a hopeless case.'

They had reached the car, and Sara took a final look backwards before getting in. She leaned back against the seat and sighed.

'I thought this charade was just to get you out of the clutches of a *femme fatale*. Now I realise how much more it is.'

'You guessed. You're very clever, Sara.'

'No, I'm not.' She looked sharply at him, sensing sarcasm, but there was none. 'It was woman's intuition—I sensed something you weren't telling me. I didn't know what it was.'

'And now you do.' He started the engine.

'Yes.' She sighed. 'Now I do.' She looked at him, but his eyes were on the road ahead. His face gave nothing away. She wanted to touch him, to stroke his skin, feel the smooth

bone structure, touch, with butterfly light fingers, his
cheeks, jawline, chin. She clenched her hands tightly. She
knew now why she loved him. She knew, and it disturbed
her.

It was past noon. Sara stood on the terrace, a glass of
champagne in her hand, looking out over the gardens to
the sea. From the dining room came the murmur of voices,
a throaty laugh, men's deeper tones, a woman's excited
squeal. She had escaped for a moment, and she breathed
deeply of the warm scented air. She wasn't used to these
people. They were not her kind, and they knew it as well.

Louise had arrived with her husband, and she had been
perfectly charming. But she made Aunt Rachel seem like
a crass beginner in the bitching stakes. Her venom was
subtler by far, the darts buried deep even before being felt.

She had swept in half an hour ago with Jack in tow and
another couple—'house guests' she had told Morgan gaily.
They were talking in the dining room, and drinking. Louise
had clearly had a few drinks before she came. She wore a
purple dress, floor-length, backless and practically front-
less as well, and she looked stunning. Jack was a tall well-
built man, silver-haired and distinguished and apparently
idolising his wife. The couple with them, an actor and his
actress wife, Nonie and Roger, were shrill-voiced and
drunk.

'So here you are. Admiring the view, dear?' Louise's
voice was silken-smooth. She materialised beside Sara, who
turned and smiled.

'Yes. Lovely, isn't it? Is yours the same?'

'More or less.' Louise looked at her. She was exactly as
Morgan had described, slim, blonde, elegant, cat-like eyes
with the faintest slant to them. Her make-up could have
been scraped off with a knife. But she was beautiful, no
doubt about that. And she hated Sara. That was equally
obvious—to Sara, perhaps to no one else.

'Well, well,' she drawled, 'Morgan's a dark horse. We had no *idea*!'

'No.' Sara looked modestly down at her glass. She didn't like Louise, and she could see precisely why Morgan didn't, but she was going to play the part of a demure fiancée to the best of her ability. 'He didn't want to say anything—before.'

'Before what, dear?'

'Before it was definite.'

'So you've only just become engaged? How *romantic*!'

'Well, just a week or so.' Sara looked her candidly in the eyes. 'I'm only nineteen, you see,' she smiled a gentle smile. 'And Morgan—well, he wanted me to be sure.'

'And are you?'

'Oh *yes*.' I should be an actress, Sara thought, trying to hide the laughter that threatened to bubble over.

'I'm so glad.' Louise turned to look into the room. Morgan was talking to Jack. 'At least one of you is.'

'What do you mean?' Wide-eyed, Sara looked at her as Louise turned back.

She received a cat-like smile. 'Oh, darling, far be it from me to disillusion you, but your *fiancé*,' the word was heavily underlined, 'is hardly the most *faithful* of men—ah! but there, he'll have told you—bared his all, I dare say, hmm?'

'I'm not sure what you mean,' Sara whispered. She put her glass down and fingered her engagement ring as if it were a talisman.

'Oh, don't take any notice of me darling! Heavens, I'm sure he'll settle down.' But she managed a doubtful, brave smile as she said it.

Sara managed to make her lip quiver. She wasn't sure how, but the threatened laughter helped. 'Please tell me what you mean,' she said very determinedly—and with an equally brave, anxious look into the shadowy room.

'You're very young, aren't you?' Louise regarded her with a sad look. 'So very young.' The words 'poor child' could well have been added. They hung there anyway.

Sara bit her lip. She was going to scream or fall down laughing in a minute if she wasn't careful. 'You mean, he's —he's—experienced?' she managed to whisper.

'I mean, my dear, he's had half the women on the Riviera.'

'Oh!' Sara put her hand to her mouth. Her eyes were like saucers. 'I don't think you should be telling me this, Louise. I mean, isn't it a bit disloyal to be talking like this?'

'I'm doing it for your own good. He'll break your heart.'

'No! I love him!' Sara declared dramatically. It was true, of course, but she wasn't the person Louise thought she was. It was getting so *complicated*. She was playing a rôle within a rôle, speaking lines written for her by someone else. She *was* someone else. She was, as far as Louise was concerned, a naïve nineteen-year-old innocent to whom Morgan Haldane had become engaged.

'I'm sure you do, darling. So do half the women round here. He doesn't bother to get engaged to them, though— you must have proved more difficult.' Louise positively purred, looking Sara up and down in a decidedly uncomplimentary manner.

'What *do* you mean?' asked Sara in horrified tones.

Louise laughed. 'Good God, what do you *think* I mean? Has he taken you to bed yet?'

'*No!* Of course not!'

'Wait till he does, dear. Then hang on to your ring. It'll be all you have left. Take it from me—I know.'

'You mean *you've* had an affair with him?' She might as well be naïve, if that's what Louise thought she was.

'I'm married!' Louise answered coldly.

Sara laughed; she couldn't help it. The laughter pealed out, bubbling up from where she had been stifling it for the past minutes. Helplessly she clung to the wall, and Louise stood there, face dark with anger, and any minute she was going to lash out, and if she did she'd be sorry because Sara was prepared to hit back, and harder.

'Sara?' It was Morgan, stepping out, amused, puzzled, looking from her to Louise and back again. Sara went over and flung her arms round him.

'Oh, Morgan! Louise has just been warning me about you! Darling, I didn't realise you were such a—a—Casanova——' she collapsed helplessly against him, and looked across at the icily angry woman who stood as if, for the moment, she didn't know what to do. 'You didn't tell me you'd hit it off with half the women on the Riviera—oh, Morgan, you are *wicked*!'

Louise stalked out, and into the house. They heard her voice, shrill, cutting, Jack's mumbled reply—then the buzz of voices. Sara looked up at him.

'Oops!' she whispered, and giggled.

'Stay there.' Morgan disengaged himself. 'Don't *move*.' He disappeared inside, and Sara stood where he had left her. Oh Lord, she thought, I think I've blown it! But she knew at that moment that there was no other way for the scene to have gone. Louise was Aunt Rachel, Elizabeth and Jeanette rolled up into one, and more. She had just had the biggest surprise of her life.'

The voices had resumed. Morgan's drink supply was apparently never-ending, and Louise's friends had their priorities. Sara could see the two standing at the table, helping themselves. She couldn't see Louise, or Jack—or Morgan. Sara looked up at the sky, then she picked up her glass and downed the contents in one go. She heard a laugh, then the actress friend drifted out, glass precariously full.

''Lo,' she said, weaving across to where Sara stood. 'Oops!' This as she spilt some champagne down her dress. 'Silly!' She drank some and smiled blearily at Sara. 'Mind if I join you?'

'Not at all.'

Nonie sat down on a chair. 'Well, ducky,' she said very

confidentially, 'I don't know what you said to Louise, but she's just had a pink fit in there. It was *lovely*!' She giggled helplessly.

'Did I upset her?' enquired Sara innocently. 'We were only having a little talk. Oh dear!'

'She's like that.' Nonie beckoned Sara and put her finger to her lips. 'Ss-shrtrickly between you n' me, ducky, she's a teeny bit jealous.'

'Oh, *no*!' Sara sat down opposite Nonie at the table. 'Oh *dear*!'

'S'true. Got a bit of a thing for your Morgan—mind you, I don't blame her.' Nonie smiled brilliantly. 'He's rather dishy.' She raised her glass. 'Here's to dishy men.'

'I do hope I haven't upset her too much,' said Sara doubtfully, biting her lip.

'She'll get over it. Hates to lose face—know what I mean? You see, she'll be out here when she's put her mask on, and it'll be as though it never happened.'

She tapped her nose in conspiratorial fashion. Sara privately doubted that, but she nodded as if in agreement. 'I do hope so,' she said.

'Oh, she will. Just wait.'

'Have you been friends for long?' Sara asked.

'Years an' years, darling.' Nonie winked. 'Just between you me and the gatepost, the best thing she ever did was marry Jack. She was a *lousy* actress.' Her voice held feeling. Sara closed her eyes. This was friendship?

'She's very attractive,' she murmured.

'Sure she is! Spends all day at the beauty parlour. She's a conceited bitch. Just take a friendly word of advice, ducky,' Nonie laid a beringed hand over Sara's, 'you're very young—don't let her get at you. She's got a tongue like vitriol—darling!' This as Louise emerged and came towards them. 'I was just talking about you! Telling Sara what old friends we are.'

Now for it, thought Sara. She wondered if Louise had

heard Nonie's words. Apparently not. Louise was smiling gently and sweetly at them both.

'Darling,' she murmured, 'we've got to go.' She gave Sara a forgiving smile. 'Jack has an appointment in Nice—a damned nuisance, but then that's business, and he's dropping Nonie and me off at the hairdresser's.'

'Oh, what a shame.' Sara stood up. Nonie was right in one thing anyway. It was as though nothing had happened—well, almost. Louise's eyes had a too bright glitter to them, and she was holding herself tightly in check. And if looks could kill, Sara thought shrewdly, I'd be all in a little heap on the ground. But on the surface, all was well.

Jack and Roger wandered out, followed by Morgan, both men kissed Sara, said they'd been delighted to meet her, and Jack added that she and Morgan must go over for dinner very soon, then the little party drifted off down the terrace to the steps, accompanied by Morgan.

She watched them go, went in and poured herself another glass of champagne, and waited Morgan's return.

She heard a car start up, then he bounded up the steps and came along the terrace. 'What happened?' he asked.

She told him, as best she could, word for word, and he smiled wryly when the recital was done. 'Hmm. She pitched in pretty strong, didn't she?'

'And have you?' she asked.

'Have I what?'

'Had half the women on the Riviera?'

He looked coolly at her. 'I wouldn't think that question even needed an answer,' he remarked.

'Oh, it's nothing to *me*,' she assured him. Funny how quickly she was learning from Louise and Nonie. 'I just wondered, that's all,' she added airily.

'Well, don't bother. You've met two typical examples. Give me credit for more taste than that!'

'Nonie wasn't bad. Considering she and Louise are such old friends, there's very little loyalty.' She repeated most of her conversation with the actress, and he laughed.

'Nice friend!'

'She fancied *you*,' said Sara. 'Said you were very dishy.'

'Did she?' he seemed amused.

'I haven't—ruined everything, have I?' she said quietly.

'I thought for one awful moment you had. But no, I think you've played it just right. You've got her bothered, Sara—and she's not used to that. She's also not used to anyone giving as good as they get. She'll be wary of you next time you meet—if they don't ask us over in a day or so, I'll have them here for dinner. And when you and she are talking, let it be known how delighted you are that Jack and I are partners.'

Sara drank her champagne. 'And that should do the trick?'

'I shouldn't be at all surprised.' Morgan looked at her. 'Have you recovered?'

'From meeting her?' She smiled. 'You know something? She didn't bother me at all. I was too busy trying to keep from bursting out laughing all the time we had our little talk to be bothered.'

'She came out to do a hatchet job on you,' Morgan told her. 'I saw her face.'

'And you let her?'

He nodded. 'I knew you'd cope, though I didn't guess how well.'

'Thanks,' she said dryly.

'Want another drink?'

'No, thanks. Three's enough for me. They can put it away, can't they?'

'That's nothing. Wait till we go to a party.'

'Are we going to?'

'Probably. The news travels fast. The phone will start ringing anytime——' as he spoke, it did. He gave her a 'see, what did I say?' look and stood up. 'Excuse me.' There were telephones all round the villa, the nearest just inside the dining room. Sara could hear his voice, not the words, only a murmur, then the ding as he replaced the receiver, and he reappeared.

'Fancy a party tomorrow?' he asked.

'Of course. Where?'

'That was a friend calling, Monique Lefevre. She's a widow—she gives the most fabulous parties, about—oh, six miles away.'

'Will Louise be going?' asked Sara.

Morgan looked at her. 'I doubt it. They don't get on.' Something in his voice made her glance sharply at him, but before she could say anything he went on: 'It's quite a *cachet* to be invited to one of Monique's parties.'

'How could she know, so soon?'

'Remember the man I saw in Paris last night? He'll be there. He'll have told her I was with a woman.'

'Did you tell her I was your fiancée?' she asked innocently.

'Yes, I did.'

'How did *she* take it?'

'Ah——' he hesitated. 'What do you mean?' accompanied by a faint frown.

'What the hell do you think I mean?' she said. Her heart sank. It was happening *again*. Just as she'd thought everything was going well, Louise met and a certain uneasy relationship established, there was this—something else. 'I mean, is she jealous? Is *she* besotted with you?'

Morgan stood up abruptly. 'Oh God,' he muttered. Sara jumped to her feet, and went over to him.

'Look,' she burst out, 'don't keep moving away when we're talking. Don't tell me *she's* another one! I mean, how many more, for God's sake? I should be on bonus or danger money or something——'

He gave a deep sigh and put his hands on her arms. 'Hold still, little wildcat! I'm not sure how to begin to tell you——'

She glared at him, breathing fire. 'This is like some bad dream,' she said. 'I don't believe it's really happening! I'm going to scream in a minute! There is something, isn't there? What *is* it?'

'She's a very lonely, unhappy woman, Sara. I've tried to help her because I feel sorry for her.'

'Answer me!' she snapped. 'Is she another one of your women?' Her eyes flashed fire. 'Oh God, I'm beginning to think Louise was speaking the truth. What do you need *me* here for? You could call up any one of your harem, and——'

'Don't be stupid,' he grated.

Sara wrenched herself free. 'Don't tell me I'm stupid!' she snapped. 'The only stupid thing I did was agreeing to come here for a holiday. Holiday! Hah!' She whirled away. 'Well, you can go to the damned party on your own!' and she turned and ran into the house, and along to her bedroom.

CHAPTER SEVEN

SARA slammed and bolted the door and went into her bathroom to rinse her burning face. She dabbed her face dry and stared at herself in the mirror. Two spots of colour blazed in her cheeks, and her eyes were large and angry.

'Damn the man!' she muttered. She had no intention of talking to him until she was cooled down. She stripped off the blue pants suit, and went in bra and pants to her suitcase to find a bikini. A swim would do the trick, a leisurely dip, and Morgan could go to hell in the meantime as far as she was concerned.

'Damn, damn,' she muttered, as she searched for the two red scraps of satin that comprised one of three bikinis Morgan had insisted on her buying. She found them and put them on the bed, and reached back to undo her bra. One of the hooks had caught, and she tugged at it, swearing under her breath the while. So much for expensive French lingerie, she thought; this wouldn't happen with trusty Marks and Sparks. 'Oh, come off, you——' she began, then froze, as an all too familiar voice said, from inches behind her ear:

'Having trouble? Let me,' and two hands were on hers. She started with the shock. She hadn't heard a sound, and whirled round.

'You!' She had forgotten the open window. He had come in—*crept* in—and surprised her. 'Get out of my bedroom!'

'I thought you might need help,' he explained.

'Not from you I don't, expert though I'm *sure* you are at helping ladies to undress.'

'Mmm.' He was looking at her bra and pants. 'Very nice.

Those I bought you yesterday?'

'*Yes*,' she hissed. 'And now you've had a good look you can *go*!'

'Oh, I've had a good look all right. I was standing outside when you stripped off. I didn't like to—er—disturb you for fear of embarrassing you, so I—er—stayed discreetly out of line.'

'You're always out of line,' she retorted with some wit.

'But when I saw you having difficulties,' he went on smoothly, as though she hadn't interrupted, 'I couldn't see you struggle.'

'I'll bet you couldn't!' Sara reached for the dressing gown she had put over a chair and put it on. It was filmy pink nylon and lace.

'I came to apologise for calling you stupid——'

'Good. Now you have. Apology accepted.' Morgan made no attempt to move, just stood looking at her, and Sara marched forward and pushed at his chest. A mistake, that. He didn't even rock on his feet, but he smiled and put his hands on her shoulders. They were cool to her burning flesh.

'I'm too big to be pushed around by a little girl,' he said softly. 'Didn't you know that? Were you going to eject me forcibly? You'll need more strength than that.'

'You're a big hulk, I know *that*,' she breathed. 'All right, so you've proved you're stronger than little me. Big deal!' she laughed scornfully. 'Remind me to give you a medal some time.'

'Temper,' he mocked. 'I'm certainly not leaving you like this. You might do something silly in the pool, like getting out of your depth.'

'Then why don't you stand and watch me? You can dive in if you see any sharks!' she snapped. 'You're good at *that* anyway.'

'What? Going after sharks?' he enquired, still gently mocking.

'No! Standing looking. Let me go!'

'Not yet. You're interesting when you're angry. No wonder Louise came in screaming for blood. I'll bet you scared her.'

'I'm obviously not having the same effect on you,' she snapped.

'Most interesting. Did you know your eyes go darker when you're mad? Nearly violet.'

'I'm delighted to hear it. I like violet eyes—and as I'm nearly always mad with you, because of all the arrogant male chauvinist pigs I've ever met you take the biscuit, and if there was a golden pig award *you'd* win it hands down— I'll probably always have violet eyes, so you'll just have to get used——'

She stopped. Morgan was laughing, silently, shaking with the effort to stem a rising tide of laughter that would have to burst out soon—'Oh!' she shouted. 'Oh, I hate you—stop laughing!' She wrenched herself free and struck out at his chest, pummelling hard, and he caught her and stopped her, took both flailing hands in his large one, and pulled her to him.

'Don't *hit* me,' he said slowly, 'or you'll get such a spanking——'

'Oh, no, you won't!' Incensed, Sara kicked out with one bare foot. It connected with his shinbone and the impact brought tears of pain to her eyes. 'Ouch!'

'Serves you damned well right, you little vixen,' he shook her. 'I've warned you about your temper——'

'Let me *go*!' Her hair tumbled wildly about her face, and her heart pounded, a mixture of fear and excitement. She struggled violently to escape, and he dragged her to the bed, sat down and pulled her over his knee.

'Don't you dare!' she shouted. 'Don't you——'

Morgan's hand descended, hard, twice, then he pulled her to her feet again. 'That's so you'll learn not to kick!'

She twisted round in his arms so that her back was to

him, and bent forward, reaching away, but he twisted her around again, pulled her tightly to him, and kissed her. Too late, just before his lips came down on hers, she saw the sparks of dark anger in his eyes—and excitement.

She knew, moments later, the truth of that excitement. Morgan was aroused in a way she had never known before, and he held her locked to him and kissed her deeply and in a way that left no doubt of his intention—and then, subtly, imperceptibly, the hard violence and anger of the punishing kisses changed. He sought her mouth again, and his mouth was no longer hard, but softer, sweeter—demanding. She felt his hands come up to her shoulders, sliding down the flimsy dressing gown, felt it slide to the floor. Then he picked her up and carried her to the bed, and lay down beside her.

She put her hands up to his face, saw what was in his eyes, and murmured something, a wordless plea, she knew not what. Then his lips were on hers again and she was drowning, lost, unheeding of anything else except what was happening to her; the warm tide of excitement pulsing through her, the tingling in the blood—the fire——

Morgan released her from the sweet imprisonment in which he held her, and his face was very dark and serious, his eyes deep pools of desire. 'Oh, my God,' he said; his voice was shaking. 'This is madness—Sara——'

She knew that too. She had the heady sense of power, of knowing him entirely, yet he had scarcely begun to make love to her. She wanted him as she had never wanted anyone. She needed him to make love to her, and she murmured softly, touched his face with trembling fingers and ached for him to take her and possess her fully. He groaned and put his lips to her hand, his tongue caressing the skin, sensuous, torturing. 'Let me go,' he whispered, and she knew that the power was hers. To touch—or to move away —and she had only to touch him, and he was lost. He was no longer the dark powerful man who had come into her life two days previously, no longer in control of every situation. Anything else—not this. It gave her a heady sense of reckless power, and she laughed softly, loving him with every part of her mind and body; she was drunk with the wild pounding in her head as he held her hand tightly and laid it to his face and rubbed his mouth against her palm in a way that made her heart beat almost uncontrollably. Yet, apart from that, he was making no attempt to caress her. It was as if some vestige of control remained. And all she had to do——

She lifted herself up slightly and looked down at him, bent to kiss him, and saw his eyes darken as she reached him. Then her mouth was on his, and her soft body moulded against his own; he put his hand up to lay behind her head and pull her ever closer until they could scarcely breathe, and breathlessly they clung together, two bodies as one, on fire, burning with a heat which only one thing would quench.

Morgan made a supreme effort, pushing her away, holding her at arm's length as he struggled to sit up, and she fell back, exhausted with desire, panting, gasping air into her lungs as he sat up and looked down at her lying there. Her bra had snapped, her breasts were revealed, round and firm, rosy-tipped, and she groaned, aching for him to touch, to hold, to take——

He moved, softly, slowly, trembling uncontrollably, his mouth on her mouth, then on her chin, her neck, kissing the tell-tale pulse, then lower, and Sara arched her back and cried out in joy as his mouth teased her breasts—and then stopped teasing——

'Ah——' then—'aah——' Bliss, sheer, formless, blurred movement and sensation. She held him, held his shoulders, feeling the tensed muscles of his arms and back beneath her hands as his mouth quested and found, sought and received an answer....

There was a roar of an engine from outside, a squeal of

brakes—a shuddering, grinding crash—then silence. Morgan, his head resting on Sara's breast, looked up, dazed, almost, it seemed—drunk.

She had gone cold. In that instant of the terrible noise from so near, she had been waiting for his next, inevitable actions, and the sound came as a horrible shocking intrusion. He stumbled to his feet and went to the window, then: 'Oh—God!' She heard his shout, then, barefoot, he was running away. Sara followed, realised her scanty clothing and whipped on her pants suit in seconds. She nearly fell over his discarded shoes by the bed, stumbled and followed the way he had gone, along by the pool, past it, to the terrace—and from there she saw the reason for the noise. A car had crashed below, past the sunken garden, gone straight into a large cypress tree, and was resting at an odd angle with its hood against the trunk.

Morgan had already reached the car, as had Martine, and a strange man. Morgan was opening the driver's door as Sara reached them. She saw him lift out a woman, say something to the man—presumably Martine's husband—who dashed off towards the sunken garage under the terrace and returned moments later with a fire extinguisher. Meanwhile Morgan was carrying the woman, a beautiful dark-haired creature who was limp and unconscious, but with no visible signs of injury. He rapped out something to Martine, who nodded anxiously and darted off.

'Can I do anything?' asked Sara.

'I'm taking her into the house. Martine's phoning the doctor. Come with me.'

'Yes, Morgan.' She turned back to look. The man had opened the hood, extinguisher at ready, but there seemed no danger of fire. Sara followed Morgan up into the kitchen, through it, up the staircase and then into a bedroom. He laid the still inert woman very carefully on to the bed and bent over her.

'Monique,' he said quietly. The only answer was a groan.

Morgan took hold of her wrist and looked at his watch. His face was as white as the unconscious woman. Sara stood there, knowing there was nothing she could do, shocked by everything that had so suddenly happened—and the greatest shock of all was to know that this was Monique, the widow, the old friend who had so recently telephoned —and then presumably driven over post-haste, so fast in fact that she had crashed. There could be—to Sara's befuddled brain anyway—only one reason for that; Monique had been unable to stay away from Morgan after hearing the news that he was engaged. She found that her hands were clenched tightly, the nails digging into the palms. Oh lord, was this the effect he had on *every* woman?

He turned to her. 'Her pulse is okay,' he said. 'I think she's only concussed. The doctor should be here soon.'

'Is there—anything I can do?'

He shook his head. 'No.'

'Did she say she was coming over on the phone?'

He rubbed his jaw as if weary and Sara saw the shock on his face. He looked like a man who was just recovering from a knock-out blow. 'No,' he said.

Sara looked at her. Louise had been beautiful, her beauty aided by cosmetics. Monique wore no make-up, and even though white and unconscious it was easy to see that hers was a beauty from within. Classic features, dark hair tumbled about her face, skin deathly white, she was beautiful. Sara felt sick at heart—and saw that Morgan was watching her. Unable to look at him, she went over to the window. Why? she thought. Why? Why should he pretend, put on this charade with *me*, try to make love to me— and he so nearly had—when it's obvious that he loves this woman? She fought back the feeling of revulsion at the memory of what had just happened in her room, and put her hand to her lips. Her body was raw with the aftermath of desire. She wished she had never met Morgan Haldane, she wished——

His hand was on her arm. She turned, eyes wide. 'Please——' she begged. It was all there in her face for him to see. She saw his face tighten, saw the flash of dark anger in his eyes, felt him take his hand away.

'It's not——' he began, only then came the sound of footsteps on the stairs, Martine's voice, calling:

'*Monsieur, le docteur est ici.*'

Morgan strode over to the door and answered her. Whatever he had been going to say was lost for ever. The doctor, a thin grave man of about sixty, came in and went over to the woman, rapping out questions to Morgan as he examined her, deftly and quickly with skilful hands.

He straightened after a few minutes. The woman on the bed was stirring, saying something that Sara couldn't hear. The doctor's voice was soothing as he answered her, in French: 'You are all right, *madame*. You are very fortunate—a slight touch of concussion, no bones broken. You will rest here for a while—no pillows, please.' He removed the pillows and lowered Monique's head. 'Monsieur Haldane, a word with you, please.' A brief glance at Sara. 'Stay with her, *madame*, if you will.'

They went out, Sara crossed to the bed, and Monique smiled faintly at her. 'You must be Sara,' she whispered in English.

'Yes. Don't try to talk.'

'I am all right. I am tough. You must—forgive me for rushing over—I came only to—see——' she winced, as if in pain, then went on: 'How stupid of me——'

'Please, don't upset yourself.' Sara sat on the bed, and in an instinctive gesture of comfort and sympathy that was over and above her feelings of sick jealousy, took the woman's hand. 'You must rest, as the doctor said. We will look after you.'

'You are very—kind, Sara. And you are very beautiful. I can see why Morgan'—a spasm of pain contorted her features for an instant—'loves you.'

But he doesn't, Sara wanted to cry. How can you be so stupid? Don't you know the truth? It had hurt her to say what she had, that was obvious. How cruel he must be! Did he want to make Monique jealous? If so, he had succeeded. He had succeeded almost too well. She had nearly killed herself. Sara hated him at that moment. And if he had entered the room then, he would have seen it, but he didn't. It was Martine who came in, followed by the doctor, who looked at Sara. 'Monsieur Haldane has gone to phone for a nurse,' he told them. 'It is better if Madame Lefevre stays here overnight. It will not inconvenience you too much, *mademoiselle*, will it?'

'Of course not.' As if it had anything to do with me, she thought wryly. 'Is there anything I can do, doctor?'

'Nothing, thank you, *mademoiselle*.' He was very formal, very correct, a thin grey-haired man with old-world courtesy. 'The nurse will attend to her needs.' Sara looked at the housekeeper. Did she know? No wonder she had been surprised when Morgan introduced her as his fiancée! She must know Monique as well—perhaps better than she knew Louise. She must be wondering.... Nothing showed in her face. She stood there, hands clasped, and listened attentively to the doctor.

'I will wait until the nurse arrives,' the doctor continued. 'And then I must depart. Perhaps, Martine, you would be kind enough to make me a coffee?'

'*Tout de suite, monsieur le docteur. Et vous, mademoiselle?*'

'*Oui, merci.*' The woman went out, closing the door. The doctor looked at Monique, who lay listening, half asleep.

'And now, Madame Lefevre, a little sedative for you, I think.' He opened his bag.

Monique managed a wry smile. 'You must think me a very silly woman,' she murmured.

He was busying himself with hypodermic syringe and capsule. 'It is foolish indeed to crash your car, *madame*,' he answered. He dabbed her arm with ether-soaked cotton wool. 'A beautiful car like that! But these things happen, alas. A good job it happened here, I think, and not on some lonely road, eh?' The needle went in. Monique never flinched. 'Rest now. You will sleep, and when you wake, a nurse will be looking after you. And try to take it easy in future, eh? Not so much dashing about?'

'I'll try. Don't I get a coffee?'

'No, you don't. You get nothing at all today. Perhaps tomorrow? I will call in again in the morning to see you.'

'But I'm giving a party tomorrow night——' she began.

'You will be giving no more of your parties for a week or two, that I can promise you!'

'You're a bully——' but her voice was weakening, the words were slurred, and she closed her eyes. The doctor took her pulse, nodded, patted her hand. Then he turned to Sara and smiled.

'She will sleep. Excuse me, I was not aware that you were Monsieur Haldane's fiancée.' He gave her a charming smile. 'I regret we meet under such unfortunate circumstances.' He came forward, took her hand and bowed. 'Dr Rambeau, *mademoiselle*.'

'How do you do.' He had switched to English, which he spoke fluently. 'Are you Morgan's doctor?'

'I am, though he rarely has need of my services.' A Gallic shrug accompanied the words, and a wry smile. 'I would be a poor man if all my patients were like him!'

There seemed no answer to that, and Sara merely echoed his smile. 'Is Madame Lefevre also your patient?' she asked.

'Yes. A very charming person.' He spared a glance at the sleeping woman. 'I am always telling her she drives too fast. Now, perhaps, who knows, she will take heed of my advice and get herself a chauffeur. Ah!' This as Martine returned with a tray, followed by Morgan, who had pushed open the door for her. 'Thank you, Martine.'

'A drop of cognac with that, Doctor?' asked Morgan.

'Ah no, a nice thought, but when I leave here I am visiting another patient. You were lucky to catch me, Morgan; I was about to leave when your call came. She will sleep for a while now. The nurse is coming?'

'She'll be here very soon.'

'Good, good. I trust it is all right for Madame Lefevre to stay? I could, of course, have her moved to my clinic if——'

'I wouldn't hear of it.' Martine had departed silently, and they drank the strong coffee, which was precisely what Sara needed. 'I've phoned her house and told them what happened. Her son is due home this weekend from school, and I'm sending Jacques to fetch him here when he arrives.'

'Poor child.' The doctor shook his head. 'Still, he will be much happier here than——' he stopped abruptly, and it seemed to Sara that he exchanged a glance with Morgan, who nodded. The doctor finished his coffee and said: 'I trust you will tell her housekeeper to let everyone know the party is cancelled?'

It had been, Sara felt quite sure, a deliberate change of subject. She wasn't imagining that exchanged look. She pondered the significance of it, only half listening to Morgan's answer. There were so many undercurrents; it was like trying to swim in a sea which swirled dangerously just under the surface, while appearing smooth. She shivered, finished her coffee and took the men's cups from them, and put them on the tray.

'I'll take this to the kitchen,' she said.

Morgan opened the door for her, and closed it after her. Sara paused in the corridor, not deliberately, but to move one cup and saucer on the tray, and heard the doctor's voice. He spoke in French, and quickly, but she picked up the words, before she moved away. 'The boy should be told the truth, in my opinion. He is old enough now——'

'He thinks his father is dead,' Morgan cut in quickly.

And Sara, unable to help herself, paused, heart hammering. She didn't normally eavesdrop, but she simply couldn't help herelf. 'Isn't that best?' His voice was hard.

'No! He is a fine boy. Would *you* not be *proud* of him? To think that she lives so near to here——'

'It's her wish.' Morgan moved away from the door, obviously nearer to the doctor, but she heard his next words before she found, at last, the power of movement. 'It is not for me to tell him the truth, you understand? *She* is his mother. Only she can decide——'

She walked, very steadily towards the stairs. Her face felt stiff and sore, as if she had been crying. Morgan was the father of Monique's son. She was also a widow. She didn't want to, but she was going to ask Martine some questions.

Martine was alone in the kitchen, preparing vegetables. Something bubbled in a pan on the large cooker, and she looked at Sara as she went in and rushed to take the tray from her. 'Ah, Mademoiselle should not have bothered!' she exclaimed.

'It was no trouble.' It hurt to smile. Sara was still numbed with shock, but she had to know. 'Madame Lefevre is sleeping, Martine. The doctor has given her a sedative. I believe her son is coming here soon. Shall I help you get a room ready for him?'

'No, *mademoiselle*. All is in order.'

'Oh, good. How—er—old is he?'

'Ten. He is always at boarding school, you understand, but comes home some weekends. A charming little boy. Bernard is his name.'

'I didn't know she had a child.' It was getting easier now. She knew she should feel ashamed at prying, but she didn't. 'How long ago did her husband die?'

'Four years ago, when Bernard was only six. They were in America then, and she returned here shortly afterwards and moved back into her villa.' Martine sighed. 'Such a tragedy! They had only been married for such a short time, six years. Monsieur Lefevre was a businessman from Paris. I met him only briefly once when Monsieur Haldane gave a party to celebrate their wedding, but he was a charming man.'

Sara's brain was calculating rapidly. Bernard was ten. Monique had married her late husband ten years ago, and he had died four years previously. She went cold at the implications. Suppose she had been pregnant with Morgan's child when she married him? If what the doctor said was true, that must be the case. There was therefore one more question. Hating herself now, she said: 'How terrible! Had she known Monsieur Lefevre long before they married?'

'Alas no, it was—how do you say—a whirlwind romance. They met and married within weeks of meeting. Monsieur Haldane arranged everything.'

I'll bet he did, Sara thought bitterly. Getting rid of an unwanted pregnant mistress was probably something he was an expert at. 'I see. I'll let you get on with your work, Martine. I think I'll go out for a walk. Will you tell Monsieur Haldane if he wants to know where I am?'

'Naturellement.' The woman nodded, smiling. 'Take care.'

'I will.'

Sara walked steadily out, along the terrace, down the steps into the sunken garden. She was beginning to understand now why Morgan ran the children's home. It was a sop to his conscience; it no doubt made him feel good. She wondered, bitterly, if any of the orphans there were his. Tears blinded her as she walked along, and she looked back at the villa; there was a blur of movement at one window and she blinked hard and the blur resolved into the figure of Morgan. He stood there watching her. Sara turned her head away. She wondered how long she could go on staying here now, knowing what she did.

CHAPTER EIGHT

IT was Saturday morning, and Sara sat by the side of the pool and watched Bernard's attempts to do the Australian crawl. She had been swimming, and was resting after a strenuous ten lengths when Bernard had appeared, a skinny dark-haired boy with laughing dark eyes, and asked if he might join her.

'It's all yours,' she told him. 'I've just swum ten lengths and I'm going to have a rest. Then I'll come back in.'

He nodded, stood poised at the end, then did a clumsy dive, all arms and legs, and surfaced laughing. 'Oh,' he cried, 'that was terrible! Did I splash you, Miss Sara?'

She shook her head, and he bobbed under and began the laborious crawl. As she watched him she thought back to the previous night, when he had arrived. She had waited, apprehensive, torn with sick doubts and aching with the knowledge of what she had learned.

They had waited dinner for him. Sara had managed to avoid Morgan by pretending a headache and staying in her room, and if she could have had dinner there as well she would have done so, but with the arrival of the nurse, and the imminent arrival of Bernard, the housekeeper had enough to do.

She had changed into a simple orange chiffon dress and gone into the dining room. She had heard a car arrive, and voices. Now she was about to meet Morgan's son. She entered the room, and they were standing at the window, looking out. Morgan had one hand on the boy's shoulder and was leaning slightly, pointing out something in the far distance. Then, hearing her, Morgan had turned.

'Is your headache better?' he had asked.

'Yes, thank you.' She looked at the boy. Tall, thin, with shaggy dark hair, he stood there looking at her with a faint, nervous smile on his face, and a quick following glance to Morgan.

'Sara, this is Bernard Lefevre, Monique's son. Bernard, this is Miss Bourne, my fiancée.'

Sara wanted to scream, to turn and run. She didn't want to stand there while this boy came forward. She hated Morgan, she hated him—no, she didn't; she couldn't. He was young, and vulnerable, and he was taking her hand shyly. He smiled, and his face was transformed. 'How do you do, Miss Bourne,' he said, in careful English. 'I am very pleased to meet you. It is—very kind of you and Monsieur Haldane to allow me to stay here with Maman.' It was a little speech, delivered slowly and with care, and he had probably been rehearsing it silently ever since he had arrived.

Sara wanted to hug him. How could you not like a boy like that, with such a natural charm? 'I'm very pleased to meet you, Bernard,' she said. 'And you speak excellent English.'

He flushed under his tan. 'Thank you.'

She recalled the scene, and the meal afterwards, at which Bernard had chatted away about school, and the things he had to tell his mother, and the evening had passed rather better than Sara could have expected.

And now he was swimming over to the side nearest her, shaking the wet hair out of his face like a puppy, and pulling himself out to sit beside her. 'Miss Sara,' he said gravely, 'may I ask you something?'

'Yes, of course.' She smiled at him. His manners were impeccable. He was clearly a well brought up boy, and he was going to be very good-looking in a few years....

'May I speak English with you all the time? Do you mind?'

'Of course not!'

He sighed a deep sigh. 'Oh, that is good. I spoke to Maman before, when I got up, and she said I was not to be a nuisance to you. But if you don't object——'

'No. You speak very well, as I told you. How is your mother?'

'Much better, thank you. The doctor will come soon, I think. I am glad that she is here. Maman's housekeeper is a bit—er—strict—with me—oh, excuse me, I should not have said that!' He looked alarmed, blushed slightly, and Sara patted his hand.

'It's all right. You mean you'd rather be here than at home, while your mother's not well? That's perfectly natural.'

He pulled a little face, relieved. 'Please don't misunderstand. Madame Hortense is very kind really—I just think she doesn't like boys of ten!' He gave her such a boyish grin that Sara began to laugh. Bernard joined in, then jumped to his feet. 'Oh, you are so *kind*, Miss Sara.'

She sobered. She didn't feel kind. If he knew what was going through her mind about his father, he would be shocked. But then he would never know, just as he would never know that Morgan *was* his father. Because Morgan didn't want it known. He denied the boy because children clearly had no place in his life—nor did a wife, she thought wryly. There would have been nothing, in the past four years, to have stopped him marrying Monique. Morgan had been right; she was not like these people. Their manners and morals were not hers. But Bernard was innocent of any blame. He was a victim.

She jumped to her feet. 'Thank you, Bernard. And for that, would you like me to teach you to dive?'

'Would you? Please?'

'I would and I will. Follow me.' They stood at the deep end of the pool, and she said: 'Okay, watch what I do. Like *this*——'

Morgan's voice came from his window, and he stepped

out, fully dressed in white tightly fitting jeans and short-sleeved black tee-shirt.

'Good morning,' he called, and Sara froze. She hadn't seen him since she had escaped after dinner.

'Good morning,' she and Bernard echoed, and the boy added, 'Miss Sara is teaching me to dive, *monsieur*.'

'So I see. But don't be too long, hey? Breakfast will be ready in fifteen minutes.'

Bernard looked at her. She said: 'Right, bend slightly forward—so—that's it. Now, legs like this——' she demonstrated. 'Body, arms in line. Right, in you go!'

He dived in. Not a bad attempt, and certainly better than his previous effort, and Sara clapped. 'Bravo,' she said, as he surfaced.

Morgan said quietly: 'I want to speak to you, Sara.' Bernard was swimming to the far end. She looked at him.

'Do you? What about?' She felt strangely numbed, as though the shocks and hurts had anaesthetised her to anything he could do. There was only so much she could take, and she had reached the limit yesterday when she had overheard the conversation between him and the doctor in the room of his sleeping ex-mistress. Did he think she was made of stone, like him? But then he didn't know she had thought herself in love with him. No more. She would guard her heart more carefully from now on. He wasn't going to hurt her again. When the business deal with Jack was completed, when that precious strip of land and the watermill were his, she would leave. She would never see him again. Even a debt of honour reaching out from the past was not strong enough to make her stay. But he didn't know the decision she had reached, nor would he until it was too late. By which time, with the mill in his possession, he wouldn't care....

'Something has happened to you, and I want to know what it is,' he said.

'I don't understand.' Bernard remained at the far end of

the pool as if sensing their conversation didn't include him. He was a tactful boy, as well as being polite. Sara felt sick. Didn't Morgan have *any* feelings about him? It made her go on more strongly: 'Nothing's happened. I'm here, I'm your fiancée, what more do you want?' and she added softly: 'And I enjoy being with Bernard, so why don't you leave us?' The silent, unspoken words she would have added hung in the air between them: We don't want you.

Morgan gave her a look of deep smouldering anger, then, without another word, turned and walked away. Sara dived in the pool as if to cleanse him from her, and swam steadily to where the boy waited. 'We'll practise a few more dives and then go to breakfast,' she said.

The doctor had been and told Morgan that while Madame Lefevre was recovering well, he would prefer her to stay where she was for a few more days; Bernard had spoken to his mother, and came down to where Sara sunbathed, and told her this, and she had nodded, and then he had added: 'And Monsieur Haldane is going into Cannes, he has just told me, and wonders if we would like to go.'

'Do you want to, Bernard?' she asked.

'If *you* do,' he said shyly, 'I would be very honoured to accompany you. I would like to buy a present for Maman, and perhaps you would advise me.'

'Of course.' She stood up. 'Give me five minutes to change.'

'I will tell him.' He scampered away and vanished into the house. Sara sighed, picked up her bag, and went in.

She and Bernard waited by Morgan's car for him to come out; he was on the telephone. Bernard had dressed in white tee-shirt and blue denim shorts and sandals. He handed Sara a wallet. 'Will you mind this for me?' he asked her.

She put it in her bag. 'Of course.' It would be nice to get away for a few hours. She had the money her uncle had given her with her, she might treat herself as well. A souvenir from Cannes.... It reminded her of the ashtray at the Home inscribed, 'A present from Blackpool.' How on earth had that got there? It made her remember also the whole purpose of her being here. The sooner she saw Louise, the better. The sooner the traps were prepared, and taken, the sooner she could leave. Then she went cold. When she left, she would take nothing of Morgan's, neither clothes, nor ring, nor pendant, nor watch. She would need money to travel back to England—she might need that hundred and ten pounds. It would be best to save it for the day.

'Just a moment,' she told Bernard. 'Wait here, I'm going to my room.' She ran off along the terrace, round past the pool and into her bedroom. Unlocking her old case, she put the money at the bottom, refastened it and replaced it in the wardrobe. There would be no temptation to spend now.

She went back, and Morgan was waiting with Bernard. 'I'm ready,' she said. He looked at her, and she smiled. She had her secrets, just as he had his. She knew his, but he would never know hers.

Morgan drove down to the road, and along, filtering into the passing traffic, overtaking, driving swiftly and well. 'We'll meet for lunch,' he told them, 'at one.'

Sara looked at her watch. Nearly ten-thirty now. That would give them two hours to wander around. Bernard looked happy, leaning over the seat from the back. 'At your hotel?' he asked.

'Yes. You'll take Sara there?'

'Yes, *monsieur*, thank you. Oh, this will be fun! I'm going to buy a present for Maman and Miss Sara is going to help me.'

'Is she? Good idea. And you, Sara, are you spending?'

'No.' She gave him a pleasant smile for the benefit of the boy.

'Nothing you want?'

'I don't think so.'

'But you've brought your money, in case?'

'No.'

Morgan took one hand from the steering wheel, fumbled in his back pocket, and handed her a wad of notes. 'Here, take these.'

She looked at them and shook her head. 'No, thanks.'

'I insist. Besides, what if you want a drink?'

'There's more than enough for a drink there,' she remarked drily. 'There's enough to buy a brewery!'

'Take it. You have an allowance anyway, didn't I tell you?' It was useless to say anything in front of Bernard, who sat there, clearly puzzled.

'Thank you,' she said. She zipped up the bundle in a compartment of her bag. There was the equivalent of about fifty pounds in francs. She would take whatever he gave her, keep a note of it, and repay it, later, from England.... When the time came to leave, it would be much easier to have ample for her needs while she found work and accommodation.

She smiled to herself, feeling a little better. She was going to spend the minimum. An ice cream, a lemonade, for Bernard and herself, but nothing more. But she hadn't seen the shops then....

They were in a small boutique crammed not only with jazzy clothes, but jewellery, perfume, toys, and Sara found herself weakening. Bernard was wandering around intent on finding just the right present for his mother, and the place was full of holidaymakers. But it wasn't quite like anywhere in England. There was a gloss about the women customers, an extra something. It shouted style, flair—money. Sara stood behind a deeply tanned Frenchwoman in front of her wearing only a brief suntop and shorts. She was very tall, slender, and was festooned with gold chains and bracelets—real gold. She half turned, and a faint thread of some expensive perfume touched Sara's nostrils.

The tan went right to the edges of the glossy blonde hair, caught casually in a blue ribbon. Her profile was to Sara as she examined a pair of earrings. The false eyelashes were at least an inch long and thick and the silver-white eyeshadow, both above and just below her eyes, glittered strangely in the sunlight filtering in. She looked attractive from a distance, but close up, bizarre. She gave Sara a withering look and pushed past her. Mmm, thought Sara, consider yourself put in your place! The woman undulated out of the shop on tottery high heels and Sara watched her go. Her eye was caught by a stand on the counter with false eyelashes, all thicknesses and lengths. Smiling a little smile, she picked up one of the boxes, nearly fainted when she had mentally translated the price, thought the hell with it, and bought them.

Bernard came up. 'Miss Sara, please look. Please come with me.' She followed him to a display of silk scarves hung on a stand. 'Do you think she would like one of these?' he asked anxiously.

Sara fingered one. 'I'm sure she would—they're beautiful. But have you enough money?'

'Oh yes. Monsieur Haldane, he very kindly gave me some extra money,' and he dug in his shorts pockets and peeled off several notes. Sara went very cold.

'I see. Well, in that case, of course——' she said.

Bernard was debating which of the wide variety of colours and designs he would choose. It was perfectly natural, of course. Why wouldn't a man treat his neighbour's son? Only Bernard wasn't just that; he was treating his own son.

A scarf was selected, paid for, put in a bag, and they walked to a pavement café and had ice cream sodas and watched the passing scene. The boats in the harbour dazzled in the sun, the traffic was thick, the day was shimmering hot. It was a beautiful place to be, and whatever else was happening, whatever kind of man Morgan Haldane was, Sara would never have come here had he not erupted into her life, how long—was it only three days ago? She thought about that as she sipped the cool sweet drink. If she could accept the situation—accept Morgan for the man he was and that he was not of her world and never would be, and make the utmost out of all the time that remained to her here, and keep her heart—and body—intact, then she would not be the loser.

A comment by Bernard, on a bejewelled poodle passing with its even more exotically dressed mistress, intruded in her thoughts, and she smiled at him, looked, agreed that indeed one saw some interesting sights, and decided that that was the best way to be. Cool, calm, collected—and smiling. She practised it now, and Bernard looked at her and grinned impishly.

'You are so pretty, Miss Sara,' he said. 'You are *very* pretty.'

'Why, thank you, Bernard.' She inclined her head graciously. She felt as if she knew this boy, which was odd, because she had only just met him. Yet she didn't know his mother; their only encounter had been brief. What was it Morgan had said? That she was lonely and unhappy? How could he *say* that, knowing that he could alter it? She felt wretchedly sad for Monique, who loved Morgan, and for the boy, who didn't know who his father really was—and for herself, who had made a big mistake, which she was going to do all she could to correct before it was too late.

'Shall we be moving on?' she asked him gently. 'I don't know where Morgan's hotel is. I hope you do. Is it far?'

'Not far, half a kilometre perhaps. It will be a nice walk for us.'

'Indeed it will.' She stood up, put her sunglasses on again—she had bought them at a chemist's shop when her eyes had begun to ache—and they set off at a leisurely pace, away from the bay, Bernard leading her, talking all the while, pointing out various landmarks, airing his knowledge, clearly happy.

They came to a large white hotel, set back from the road, with a car park full of Rolls-Royces and Mercedes, and Sara was about to walk past it when Bernard giggled and caught her arm. 'We are here, Miss Sara,' he said.

'Here? This—are you joking, Bernard?' she said.

'No!' He laughed delightedly. 'Really, this is Monsieur Haldane's hotel.'

My God, it's huge, she thought. A uniformed doorman eyed them warily as they walked towards the entrance. Her heart sank. She would give him one more chance. 'Bernard, if you're joking—it's very funny, and I appreciate the joke, but——'

'No, no.' He tugged her arm. Then, to the doorman, in rapid French, 'Monsieur Haldane awaits us.'

'Ah.' The wary look was switched off to be replaced by an ingratiating smile. He ran up the steps and waited to usher them through the revolving door, and bowed.

They walked in, and Morgan was waiting for them. He came across. The second surprise was the man with him. It was Jack, Louise's husband.

Over lunch at a corner table in a large air-conditioned dining room, Morgan explained that he had bumped into Jack and invited him to eat with them. Sara had spoken only briefly to him at the villa the previous day, found him pleasant, but that was all. Now, over the leisurely and superb meal, she discovered him to be an interesting and witty man. It seemed to her as if, without Louise, he was much different. He entertained her and Bernard with tales of the adventures he had had as a young man in the Merchant Navy, and the boy was enthralled. Sara found herself watching him as he spoke, his face alight as he told them what had happened one evening in a Singapore restaurant. She suspected that the story was fairly well censored, for the boy's benefit, but it was still hilarious. Jack was a handsome man, grey-haired and distinguished, with a small moustache, immaculately dressed in pearl grey suit and tie, his long fingers expressive as he drew pictures in the air of the giant cage which housed a parrot which had belonged to the proprietor of the restaurant.

'—until one of my friends crept in to bring the parrot out,' he finished, 'and found it was a *stuffed* one! Choo Ling had a tape recorder of parrot talk, and played it all the time—Jim got the shock of his life when he found the parrot was fastened to the perch!'

Bernard nearly fell off his chair. Sara rescued him just in time and looked across at Morgan. He was watching the boy with a very strange, serious expression on his face, not joining in the laughter, just watching.

'Oh, Mr Barron, you are so funny,' Bernard said.

'Well, thank you, young man,' Jack smiled. 'Don't forget to tell your friends when you get back to school.'

'I won't, sir.' He looked round the huge room, eyes like saucers. 'This is a lovely place, *monsieur*, and the meal is superb. I am enjoying myself very much.'

'That's good. I'll tell the chef,' said Morgan. His eyes were upon Sara, and he raised his glass. 'More wine, Sara?'

'No, thanks. I've had enough.' She shook her head.

'You must both come over for dinner soon,' said Jack. 'Louise was saying how much she'd enjoyed meeting you.' He told the lie blandly and pleasantly. She wondered what Louise had *really* said.

'Thank you, we'd like that, wouldn't we, Morgan?'

'Indeed yes, we would.' Morgan refilled Jack's glass. 'Could I ask you a favour, Jack?'

'Name it.'

'I've got to leave my car here. The damn thing started missing after I'd left Sara and Bernard, so Jules in the garage here is going to look at it. Could you give us a lift back?'

'Certainly. When? After the meal?'

'If that suits you.'

'Louise is having a beauty treatment—God knows why—and I've a couple of hours free, so say the word, dear boy.'

'That's fine. I've got one or two things I'd like to discuss anyway.'

They drifted out some time later, and into Jack's Rolls which waited in the car park. The drive back was accomplished in record time, and Jack parked the car near the tree where Monique had had her crash, and they went in via the terrace.

'Will you excuse me?' said Sara. 'I won't be long,' and she gave them all a brilliant smile—and escaped to her room.

It was a boiling hot day. She showered, changed into a cotton sundress and experimented with the false eyelashes before returning to see Bernard sitting alone on the terrace.

'Hello,' she said. 'Have they left you?'

He smiled at her, stood up politely to pull out a chair for her, then sat down again. 'Martine is bringing out drinks for us,' he told her. 'Monsieur Barron and Monsieur Haldane have gone up to see my mother.'

'Oh, I see.' She put her sunglasses on and sat back comfortably. She was not going to let *anything* bother her. She was not——

Morgan appeared, followed by Martine carrying a tray of glasses and a bottle of wine. He sat down, and as Martine left, poured out two full glasses and one half full, which he handed to Bernard.

'Where is Monsieur Barron?' the boy enquired.

'Talking to your mother. I came down to look after you and Sara.'

'Oh.' The boy sipped his wine politely. 'Does Maman know Monsieur Barron?'

'Oh yes. He was a friend of your grandfather's, Bernard.

They are talking over old times. It is nice for her to have visitors, isn't it?'

'Yes. I have never met Monsieur Barron before, but he is very pleasant.'

'Indeed he is.' Morgan raised his glass. 'I've known him for quite a while as well.' He looked across at Sara. 'You're not drinking.'

She picked up her glass. 'I am now.'

'When do you go back to school?' asked Morgan.

Bernard pulled a face. 'Monday.'

'How would you like to stay here for a few days? Until your mother is better?'

The boy's face lit up—then fell. 'I'd love it—*mais c'est impossible, monsieur*.' In his disappointment he lapsed into French.

'No, it's not. I've had a word with your mother. It only needs a phone call from me to your headmaster—would you like me to?'

'Oh—*yes*! Will you?' Bernard's eyes shone, and he looked at Sara. Then, almost it seemed without thinking, he grasped her hand. 'May I stay, Miss Sara?'

She laughed. 'Of course. I'd be delighted.' She spoke the simple truth. The boy's obvious affection for her was heart-warming. His hand held hers tightly, and she was well aware that Morgan had noticed. It might do him good, stir his conscience a little. It might make him think about his responsibilities. She realised the implications of her thoughts a moment later.

'Then that's settled. We'd better send you home for some more clothes, hadn't we? Go and ask Jacques to take you.'

Bernard jumped up. 'Thank you!' And he ran off.

Sara sat very still and sipped her wine.

'Well?' said Morgan softly.

'Well what?' she met his gaze blandly.

'What are you thinking?'

'Nothing that would interest you,' she said.

'I think it would.'

'Do you?' She kept a cool smile on her face. 'That's nice.'

'I'd like to see inside your head some time,' he said. The words were on one level, the emotions on another. The words were banal; what went beneath was anything but. Sara was aware of the tension stretching between them, taut as a drawn bow.

'You wouldn't like what you saw,' she retorted levelly. 'Not one bit.'

'Meaning?'

'Meaning just what you want it to mean.' Her glance was cool and controlled.

'You haven't forgotten our agreement?'

'Indeed no. It's in the forefront of my mind at every waking moment. Is that why you invited Jack for lunch?'

'Partly.'

'What was the other part?' she asked.

'It wouldn't interest you.'

'Try me,' she breathed.

'I wanted to—talk to him.'

'You're not doing so now. He's talking to Monique.'

'True.'

'Tell me,' she said in conversational tones, 'would he be visiting Monique if Louise were with him?'

'I doubt it.'

'Ah!'

'What does "ah" mean?'

She swallowed some more wine, and held her glass out. Morgan refilled it. 'Nothing,' she said. 'Merely an observation.'

'Perhaps you should observe less and see more,' he said, and the words didn't make sense to her. She felt muzzy. She had drunk a few glasses of wine at lunch, and now this. She wasn't used to drinking, particularly not at midday. Her head throbbed gently and insistently.

'I think I'll go and lie down for a few minutes,' she said, looking deep into her glass before emptying it.

'That might be a good idea,' he commented.

'Alone.'

'What else?'

Sara stood up. The terrace swayed gently. She looked around her; she wasn't sure which way she had to go. She bit her lip, and Morgan stood up and took her arm. 'It's this way,' he said.

'Thank you,' she answered, with great dignity. 'I did know.'

'I didn't think you did.'

She walked away from him, collided with a stone urn filled with plants, and went on. He followed and took her arm again. 'Follow me,' he said. 'I know a short cut.'

And he led her round the outside of the villa, past the pool, and to the arched window which she had left open.

'Thank you,' she told him. 'I can find my way now.' But he didn't seem to hear her, for he still had hold of her arm, and he guided her into her room and sat her down on the bed.

'Sit very still,' he said. 'I'm going to get you something.' And he vanished.

Sara sat very still. She had discovered, in the past few minutes, that it was far easier to obey than to think. If she tried to think, her head began to ache. If she just sat there, it was all right.

She saw Morgan come in, carrying a glass, which he handed to her, then held out his hand and put two white tablets into her palm. 'There,' he said. 'Put those in the water and watch them fizz, then drink.'

Obediently she did so. 'I think,' she said, when she had finished, 'I think I feel——'

Morgan sat beside her on the bed. 'What?' he asked.

'I don't know.' She shook her head. 'Oh! Ouch!'

'You'd better lie down.' His voice was very soothing. He

pushed her gently back and she didn't resist. She felt him take off her sandals.

Her head was whirling. 'Oh!' she moaned.

'What is it?'

'I don't know. I feel—strange.' She did—but there was an inner core of sanity. She wanted him to hold her. 'Don't —leave me——' she murmured.

'All right, I won't.'

She felt his hand on her forehead, and moaned softly. 'Oh——!'

'Do you feel ill?' His voice held concern.

'I don't know.' It was a whisper, a little whisper.

'Lie still.' Morgan was sitting on the bed. She felt the weight shift as he moved.

She shivered. 'Hold me, help me.'

She heard a faint exclamation, then she felt his arms go around her, heard his voice, in her ear. 'Like that?'

'Yes——' a mere whisper of sound. 'I'm so cold,'

'You're cold?' incredulously.

'Yes.' She shivered. She was—cold, vulnerable. Want-ing—him. Incredibly, wanting him.

She felt his weight, now beside her, and his arms around her. 'Is that better?' he asked.

'Mmm.' She was drowsy, and safe.

'Then sleep,' he whispered. 'Sleep, my love.'

CHAPTER NINE

'My love,' he had said. 'My love.' Sara closed her eyes, feeling safe now that he held her. This was all she ever wanted, to be in Morgan's arms—and was it so wicked, wanting that?

She wanted to tell him that she loved him, for even though she knew she mustn't, she did. Even in spite of all she knew about him, she loved him, and maybe, when she was sober, she would realise the folly of it, but now it didn't seem important.

She snuggled into his arms, gave a deep happy sigh, and dozed off. She slept for only a few minutes, but it did wonders. She stirred, opened her eyes, and he was lying beside her, quite still, eyes closed. He wasn't sleeping, she knew that by his breathing. She wondered what he was thinking about. Her head had stopped aching, and although she still felt pleasantly dazed from an excess of wine, it was a nice warm feeling. She was certainly no longer cold. She was very comfortable resting in the protection of Morgan's strong safe arms. For a few delicious moments she allowed herself the fantasy of imagining that they were married, and could sleep together like this whenever they wanted. It was heady and disturbing, so much so that she sat up. 'I'm all right now,' she said. She looked at him. She was mad! After what had happened yesterday—here—when she had vowed never to let him near her again, she had allowed him to lead her here, in a less than sober state, lay her down and take off her sandals—and she had actually *asked* him to hold her. She remembered that with painful clarity.

'Are you? That's nice. But don't run away yet.' He

reached out and encircled her wrist with his fingers. 'Because we're going to talk, you and I.'

'No, we're not.'

'I think we are. In fact I'd take a bet on it, because I'm not going to let you go until we've talked.'

'You're taking advantage of me because I'm—not quite strong enough to fight,' she protested.

'Mmm, very true,' he agreed, and smiled at her from the pillow, his eyes nearly black in the shadows of the room. 'So let's get on with it right away, shall we? Then we can go.' He sat up, put his arm round her shoulders in a gentle but effective imprisonment, and said: 'Talk.'

'About what?'

'You and—us—them—anyone you want.'

'There's nothing to say.' She wished he would release her. It was very difficult to think rationally when he was holding her.

'Then I'll start you off. You've behaved in a decidedly odd manner ever since Monique arrived.'

Sara caught her breath. 'She arrived, in decidedly odd circumstances, at a—v-very awkward time,' she managed to get out. Her heart was doing little flips of apprehension. Good grief, didn't he *remember*? Was *that* how little love-making meant to him?

'That's not what I mean. Don't twist my words round,' he went on relentlessly. 'You act as if I'm some kind of leper —a walking no-go area—and I saw your face when Bernard arrived.'

'I was looking at him to see if he looked like *you*!' she burst out. She had said it. She had said the awful words she hadn't intended to say. She sat rigid, feeling the release from pressure as Morgan took his arm away and stood up. He walked a couple of steps, turned, and looked down at her. Amazingly he didn't look angry. Even more astounding, he looked amused. She gazed at him, stunned, scarcely able to believe her senses.

'Ah,' he said, and nodded. 'At last! I thought so.'

Sara turned her head away. 'Oh God, you make me sick,' she whispered. 'How could you—how could you laugh——'

She was held, gripped tightly and pulled to her feet, made to face him. 'Because, you little fool,' he gritted. 'you've got it so wrong that it's almost funny. Don't you know? Can't you see?'

'I only know what I heard—overheard—when the doctor came. I only *know* that Monique was upset about us being engaged——'

'Sara,' he said, 'I'm not Bernard's father. Do you really believe I'm the kind of man who could father a child and then deny him?' His eyes blazed into hers. Now, now, at last, he was angry.

'What else could I think?' she whispered.

'I told you before, you should observe less, and *see* more. You'd better sit down; I have a lot to tell you. It won't take long, because soon we must go and find Jack, and see if Bernard has returned from his home. And when you do see them, look well at both of them, and tell me if you have anything more to say.'

Sara went very still as his words sank in. Then she looked up at him, slowly, the dawning realisation of what he was saying showing in her eyes, in her face. Morgan nodded very slowly. 'Oh yes,' he said. 'Now at last you see the truth. Bernard's father is Jack.' He pushed her gently down on to the bed, sat beside her, and took her hand. 'Any questions?' he asked.

'Does—Jack *know*?'

'No, he doesn't. And Monique will never tell him.'

'Dear God! I thought—it was—you.'

'I know you did. I put two and two together and got an interesting result. But you see, you were wrong, so very wrong. I'll tell you now exactly how wrong you were. Monique and Jack loved one another, twelve, fourteen years

ago. They had a wild, tempestuous affair that settled into
a steady relationship. I'm very fond of them both, as you'll
have gathered, but I am *not*—as I suspect you seem to
think—in love with Monique, nor have I ever been. I love
her as a brother. Then, eleven years ago, something happened. I don't know what, and I don't want to know,
because it's none of my business, but I was around when
it happened. They had a fight as wild and stormy as their
life had been—and the next minute it seemed Jack had
met Louise, fallen like a stone for her, and Monique was
left high and dry—and pregnant. She'd only just found out
at the time they quarrelled—and she swore me to secrecy.
Then, within days, she met Lefevre. He was a lonely, shy
man, a wealthy recluse—she met him by the very simple
expedient of crashing her car into his. She's always been
the most appalling driver, and I suspect she was drunk at the
time. He fell for her; she was, and is, a beautiful woman.
She told him everything, but it made no difference. He
wanted to marry her and be a father to her child. They
married, went off to America, and as far as I know were
happy for six years, until Lefevre died. I think he knew
that he was dying when they married. It was, perhaps, a
last chance of happiness for him—whatever the reasons,
it worked. Bernard had a father, legally, Monique was
secure for life. She came back here, because this is where
she was born—but she's scrupulously avoided Jack. She
could have had an abortion very easily, but she didn't because she really wanted that child—and she loved Jack.
She's always loved him, and she still does, and I dare say
she always will. Because she knows that he loves Louise,
and she wants only to see him happy, she's never told Jack
the truth.'

Sara remained motionless. She was shaken beyond words
by what Morgan had just told her.

'Now, do you *see*?' he said quietly.

'Yes. Thank you for telling me. I thought, when I saw

her dismay at meeting your fiancée, that it was *you* she loved.'

'She was dismayed for quite a different reason. She knows about Louise's feelings for me—before I had a chance to tell her the truth of our engagement, which I intended to do, she had hoped, I suppose, and this is only my own supposition, that if I had an affair with Louise, Jack might see the truth about her at last.'

'Oh!' Sara clasped her hands. 'Oh, what a mess!'

'It is. I regret not telling her—but——' he shrugged, 'perhaps it's as well she's here. She's had a chance to see Jack again.'

'Will she have told him? About Bernard, I mean?'

'No. She never will.'

'Oh God, what a waste!' sighed Sara.

'It is indeed——' Morgan paused, as Jack's voice could be heard, distantly, calling his name. 'Stay there, I'll go and see him. Have a rest if you want.'

'I don't need one now, I'm—wide awake.' She stood up. 'Morgan, I'm sorry. I'll go and see Monique. I'll tell her about our "arrangement" if you like.'

'Don't say too much. She doesn't know about the Home. You're the only person who knows. Imply that it's a business arrangement. I'll explain to her later.' He ran his fingers through his thick black hair. 'God! Louise causes more trouble than anyone has a right to——' he opened the door. 'Won't be a second, Jack.' Then to Sara, 'Come out when you're ready.' He went out.

Sara went over to the open window and looked out at the still water of the pool. Jack was Bernard's father, not Morgan. She leaned against the wooden archway, and her mind was in a turmoil. She wondered if Morgan's car had really broken down. She wondered how Jack could be so obsessed with a woman as selfish as Louise when the woman who truly loved him, and had for years, was only a few doors away. She wondered why people were so blind and stupid. She wanted to weep, but she wasn't going to. It was nothing to do with her, and soon, when she left, their lives wouldn't be any more concern to her. For she must leave, before it was too late to retrieve her heart.

She went back into her room and combed her hair, applied more lipstick, and opened her door, then took a deep breath and went to find Morgan and Jack.

The following day, Monique was allowed up. She sat at the side of the pool watching Bernard swimming with Sara, applauding his efforts as he dived to show her how well Miss Sara had taught him.

'Jolly good!' she called, as he emerged dripping and ran over to her. 'But go and ask Martine for a drink, will you, darling. Anything cool.' She smiled over at Sara. 'Is that all right, Sara?'

'Of course,' Sara laughed, and as Bernard darted off, she came out of the water and sat near Monique, dangling her feet in the pool, leaning back to taste the sun. 'Mmm, gorgeous day!'

She had had no opportunity to speak to Monique about the engagement. After Jack had left the previous day, some friends of Morgan's had arrived, talked a while, visited Monique, and ended up spending the evening drinking at a kind of impromptu party at which Sara, much to her surprise, had been star guest. The friends were Americans, two married couples, friendly and charming and totally informal. They were also friends of Monique's. The 'party' had ended after midnight, when Sara, who had carefully drunk only one glass of wine all evening, had gone to bed very sober, and rather surprised to find that she had had a very pleasant evening. There were no pressures, no act to carry out, no pretending. Morgan had been kind and loving towards her, the gleam in his eyes that only Sara could see betraying their shared knowledge of the charade.

Now, at nearly noon on a glorious Sunday morning, she

relaxed by the pool and waited for Bernard's return. Morgan had gone out an hour or so previously, mentioning something vaguely about the hotel. She wondered if he had gone to the Home. If he wanted to tell her, he would. If not, it didn't matter.

'Sara, may I ask you something?' asked Monique suddenly. Sara turned slightly. 'Of course. What?'

'When are you and Morgan planning to get married?'

Oh Lord, why wasn't Morgan here? thought Sara. 'Well,' she began, 'it's—er—difficult, Monique. You see, there's something I ought to tell you—'

Bernard reappeared bearing a tray, concentrating on not dropping it. Sara took it from him, and Monique said: 'Bernard *chéri*, go to my room, will you, and bring me a handkerchief?'

'*Oui, Maman.*' He ran off obediently, and Monique said, clearly misunderstanding Sara's hesitation:

'Do forgive me. It is a very personal question. I had no right to ask you, but I was curious. I should not have——'

There was time, if she spoke quickly. 'Monique,' said Sara, 'it's not that—only Morgan means to tell you. We're not really engaged—we're only pretending for a while—it's to do with something in business with Jack and Louise.'

Monique's face was a picture. 'Truly?' she gasped. She put her hand to her head. 'I don't understand—you seem so very suited——'

'We didn't meet until four days ago, Monique. My father and Morgan's father were working together during the war. I didn't even know of his existence before he turned up at the house where I was staying. The following evening I was here as his fiancée.'

'*Mon dieu!*' Monique looked at her stunned. '*C'est incroyable!*'

'I know it's unbelievable, but it happens to be true.' Sara moved to sit beside the older woman. 'I'm sorry if I've shocked you, but Morgan wanted you to know the truth.'

'Thank you for telling me,' Monique gave a wry smile. 'So—no wedding? *Quel dommage!*'

Sara gave a wry smile. 'No, no wedding. Once the—business matter is sorted out, the engagement will be quietly broken, and I'll return to England.' She met the other's eyes frankly. 'That's where I belong.'

'Ah, Sara, I don't know what to say.' Monique gave a sigh. 'It is time Morgan got married.'

There was absolutely nothing that Sara could say to that, and she didn't try. Then Monique began to chuckle softly. 'Oh *la*!' she said. 'Do forgive me, but I'd love to see Chantal's face when she returns from holiday and finds Morgan betrothed.'

'*Pardon?* Chantal? Who—is—she?'

Monique sobered. 'Has he not mentioned her?'

'No.'

'She is a very spoilt little rich girl who lives a kilometre or so west of here with her mother in a villa that makes mine look like a garden shed.'

'And is she after Morgan as well?' Sara asked, heart sinking.

'*And* her mother! Chantal is—let me see—twenty-two, her *maman* is about forty, a very wealthy divorcee—and they are both away in Bermuda at the moment. I think Madame Vandel had great hopes for herself, or her daughter, with Morgan.'

'Is *everyone* after him?' Sara asked drily, and Monique laughed.

'He is a most attractive man—and there aren't so many about, alas! They won't like you very much.'

'Thanks,' said Sara. She gave Monique a little grin. 'You make me feel good. First Louise tried to annihilate me—now, it seems, there are another two to watch.'

'You'll cope, I'm sure.' Monique gave a lazy smile. 'I hope we can be friends, while you are here.'

'So do I. I need a woman on my side,' agreed Sara wryly.

Monique laughed. 'Then you have one!' And she held out her hand. They shook solemnly, sealing the bargain. Sara had a brief twinge of regret for the jealous thoughts she had had about Monique. She was genuine, warm and kind. Jack must be stupid to have let her go—and even more so to have chosen Louise to take her place.

Bernard returned with his mother's handkerchief, was thanked, and dived in the pool again, watched by the two women. It was nearly lunchtime. The day stretched ahead, golden and warm and languorous.

'Can I ask you something, Monique?' asked Sara.

'*Naturellement.*'

'What do you *do* all the time?'

Monique frowned. 'I am not sure what you mean.'

'I mean—living here, in Cannes. It's beautiful, and the weather is perfect—but don't people get bored?'

'Ah, I see. Yes, there is a danger of that. That is why we give so many parties. It gives us something to do. There is a close social *clique*, as you will find out soon. And some have yachts, of course, and go sailing—but yes, life can get stale. How astute of you to realise it—not many do. We see the holidaymakers envying us, and they are here for their fortnights or a month and they go everywhere and see everything, then go home and tell everyone how perfect it is, but they don't know us at all. For the men it is different,' she gave a graceful shrug. 'People like Morgan, or—Jack,' there was a slight hesitation before the name, 'because their lives are very busy making money and more money. But if you married Morgan you would soon find yourself on the social merry-go-round—I am speaking frankly, you understand, because I feel you are honest enough yourself to want me to—but the rich life is very overrated.'

If you married Morgan, she had said. The very thought was enough to send a slight shiver right down Sara's back. How could she be bored being married to *him*? Life would be bliss——She found to her horror that she was being watched by Monique, who looked puzzled.

'Oh—sorry.' Confused, she felt her face go pink. Monique gave a very slight smile.

'My dear,' she said softly, 'don't fall under his spell. Don't let him break your heart.'

'I'm—trying not to,' Sara murmured.

'But it is difficult, *n'est-ce pas?* I am surprised he should consider such an—arrangement. I am very fond of Morgan, do not mistake me, he is a truly loyal friend, and he has been—how do you say it?—a tower of strength during a difficult time for me, but no woman has ever held his heart, and, I suspect, none ever will. He is a man alone, a man apart from others, strong and tough and independent.'

'You're not telling me anything I hadn't already guessed,' cut in Sara in dry tones.

Monique sighed. 'Perhaps not. And yet I thought, when I heard he was engaged, that at last the miracle had happened. Alas, it is not so.' She shook her head. 'And yet you look so—right together, somehow, Sara.'

But she must also feel relieved at hearing the truth, because perhaps there was a chance for her....Nothing of this showed on her face, and Sara knew she must not reveal her own knowledge of Bernard's parenthood. Oh what a muddle! The conversation only served to make her realise how far apart her world was from Morgan's.

She gave a wry look at Monique after her last words, and they seemed to echo within her, you look so right together—which only proved how deceptive appearances could be. 'Perhaps,' she said lightly. 'Morgan would look right with any woman.'

'True!' Monique laughed. 'He is an asset, no? All the hostesses giving their parties try to get him to them—if he went to all the functions he was invited, he'd never get any work done, or have any sleep.'

'I'm sure——'

Morgan was walking towards them from the terrace, and Sara's heart leapt at the sight of him. She didn't know why the effect should be heightened when he was dressed all in black, as he was now, but it was so. Tight black corduroy jeans and thin black silky sweater with roll neck, the sleeves pushed up to the elbow on tanned and powerful forearms.

'Lunch is about to be served,' he said. 'Bernard, aren't you hungry?'

'*Oui, monsieur!*' Bernard dived in and swam from the far end, and Morgan leaned over to haul the dripping boy out.

'Then I suggest you get dried,' he grinned at Monique and Sara. 'A little ride out for us this afternoon is in order, I think—and *I* will drive.' This with an eyebrow gently raised at Monique, who pulled a face.

'No need to remind me, Morgan. I have finished with driving. Does that satisfy you?'

'If you keep to it, yes,' he answered. 'Let me help you up.'

'I'll go and dress,' Sara began, and he said:

'Eat as you are. We're lunching outside.'

'Where are you taking us, *monsieur*?' asked Bernard.

'Wait and see.'

They walked slowly along, past the pool, to the terrace, where Martine was setting out plates and cutlery. The heat was intense, and Sara was already dry, her skin prickling as the golden rays tanned her. She stretched like a cat before she sat down, saw Morgan's amused look, and smiled at him. Keep smiling, she thought, it's the only way. You can't cry when you're laughing.

She watched Morgan as lunch was served. He was, no doubt about it, the perfect host, seeing that they all had sufficient. Sara, for some reason, wasn't particularly hungry, but knew better than to say so. When they had finished she left them to go and get changed.

She had put on a cool sundress, pale cream with thin shoulder straps and low scooped neckline, and was brushing her hair when a tap came at her window and Morgan stood there. 'May I come in?'

'You almost are,' she responded lightly. '*Do* come in.'

He stepped in, always a quiet mover for such a big man, she had noticed that before, and came over to where she sat at the dressing table. 'Monique says you've told her of our arrangement.'

'Yes. I thought it—appropriate. You see, she asked when we intended getting married. I couldn't tell lies, could I?'

'No. You did the right thing, Sara.'

'And in return, she told me about Chantal and her mama.' She stood and turned to face him. Sitting with her back to him, talking to him in a mirror put her at a disadvantage. She gave him a sweet smile.

'Good grief, did she?' he exclaimed.

'Yes, she did. I asked you before, remember?' she persisted.

'So you did. But they're hardly going to be any concern——'

'Monique seems to think so,' she retorted smartly.

Morgan shrugged. 'That's her opinion. Just think of them as Aunt Rachel and Elizabeth.'

'There couldn't be two of *those*!' she burst out. What a thought!

'No. But you'll cope as admirably——'

'As I did with Louise? Thanks! You have more faith in my capabilities than I!'

'No. I'm realistic.' He gripped her by the shoulders, quite gently. 'You're tougher than you look.'

'The opposite of you,' she murmured.

'What does that mean?'

'Work it out.'

'I look tougher than I am?' he questioned.

'Yes. I think you're a coward, if you must know. You saw in me a chance to give the big brush-off to all your *devoted* female hangers-on. There's just one snag, Mr

Clever Haldane. They'll all be rushing round like wasps to a honey jar the minute I leave, to "comfort" you!'

He wasn't laughing now. His face was quite serious. 'Then,' he said softly, 'we'd better extend the arrangement, hadn't we?'

'What does *that* mean?' she echoed his question.

'Consider it as a "job"—for as long as necessary.'

'As necessary?' she said, voice rising. 'What the hell does that imply? Till they all die of old age? No, thanks—I'm leaving here just as soon as you've got Louise sorted——'

'For a few more months——' he continued, as though she hadn't interrupted him. 'Until I think of a better plan.'

'Hah! I'm sure you'll do that all right. It's only a pity you didn't before. You're a scheming, conniving, crafy man! I'll bet there was nothing wrong with your damned car yesterday—I'll bet you made that move to get Jack here talking to Monique.'

'Lower your voice,' he snapped. 'Do you want everyone to hear?'

'Damn everyone!' she sparked back. 'You don't deny it?'

'No.' He smiled reminiscently. 'It worked, didn't it?'

Sara was shaken by the cool admission. It had been a shot in the dark. Silenced for a moment, she stood there, and Morgan took advantage of her silence to say:

'We'd work well together, you and I. Our minds are of a wavelength——'

'There's no one got a mind like yours!' she snapped. 'And if you're so fed up with the attentions of all these women why don't you tell them you've lost all your money? They'd disappear like snowflakes in the sun!'

'Poetic too? Beautiful!'

'Don't patronise me,' she grated, and pulled herself free of his grasp.

'I'm not. You're damned prickly, Sara. You want to watch that.'

'Well!' she gasped. 'You take the biscuit! You're aggressive, bossy, and you have the nerve to tell me I'm prickly! There's nothing wrong with *me*, chum. Nothing at all.'

He began to laugh—deep, amused, his face transformed. Sara whirled away from him, incensed. 'Don't laugh at me!' she yelled, and looked for something to throw at him—but he came after her, caught her, and pulled her round.

'You're magnificent,' he said, when he could speak. 'You're a walking firecracker, you know that? Life could never be dull with you around.' She stopped struggling, looked at him, her hair tousled, cheeks pink, bosom heaving.

'I'm not here for your entertainment,' she said.

'Then how would you like to be my social secretary? A hundred pounds a week—or the French equivalent, all board, chauffeur-driven car, and complete freedom to go where you want, with one proviso.'

She was stunned. Her mouth fell open, and he put his hand on her chin and lifted it gently, shutting it. 'A nod will do,' he said helpfully.

'A hundred——'

'So you agree? Good. Don't you want to know what the proviso is?' he asked. When she didn't answer, he added: 'No men. I mean—officially—we'll be engaged.'

Sara's mind was working rapidly, and she scarcely heard his words, and they certainly didn't register. One hundred a week, five thousand two hundred if she stuck it for a year, enough to get herself a comfortable apartment in London or near, and look around for a job with no financial worries—and all she had to do was keep out of love with him for twelve months.

'Hmm? You agree? And you'll have free rein to get rid of Chantal and her mama, and the others——'

'What others?' she said feebly. The whole thing was turning into some sort of bizarre dream. She was quite

sure she was awake, and she had had no more than one glass
of wine at lunch, but the situation was as unreal as a misty,
half-remembered-on-waking type of dream. Morgan released her and stepped slightly back.

He shrugged. 'Oh, nothing to worry about.'

'What others?' she demanded. She glared at him, arms
akimbo, and advanced on him. His mouth trembled as
though with suppressed fear—or laughter. She didn't think
it was fear.

'Various socialites—all boring and brittle,' he told her.
'Not my types at all.'

'Name one,' she demanded.

'Er—well, let me see—Andrea Smythe-Forbes—*Lady*
Andrea—expatriate Englishwoman, divorced, terribly upper
crust—you know the type.'

'No, I don't, actually,' she smiled sweetly. 'And I'm to
be your social secretary—unofficially, of course. Tell me,
why do you stay here if you find them so damned boring?'

'Because I have an obligation, remember?' he said softly.

She had forgotten about the nuns and the children, actually forgotten, for the moment. 'Oh,' she said, equally
softly.

'So, for *them* if not for me, will you?'

She was weakening, she knew it. Unfortunately, so did
he. He went on: 'It will give me more time—and once I
get the land, and start with the building alterations, I'll be
fully occupied. I need you, Sara, don't you see?'

He needed her. He said it simply. Perhaps he did. He
needed her as a buffer against the social whirl. She would
soon be known as that possessive bitch who'd managed—
God knows how—to entrap the magnificent Morgan Haldane—and they'd wonder how she'd done it, and only she
and Morgan, and possibly Monique, would know the truth.
She started to laugh, softly at first, helplessly, until the tears
ran down her cheeks. Morgan caught hold of her and she
told him why she was laughing, then he joined in, and they

clung together—and she knew, painfully, that it was already too late, much, much too late. No chance of saving her heart from this skilful assault—it was lost already.

'Will you?' he said at last.

She nodded. 'I don't think I've any choice,' she murmured, and sighed, and pushed him gently away. She looked at him, at the dark strength of him, the virile aura he exuded, and she knew, beyond any shadow of doubt, that it wasn't only going to be her heart that he would possess before the time was out. There was a sense of inevitability about it. She shivered inwardly, deliciously, briefly fearful that it must show in her face, and turned slightly away, lowering her eyes.

Morgan took hold of her chin and tilted it to face him.

'You won't regret it,' he said, and the room was filled with that shimmering thread of tension, wrapping round them, filling them both. He caught his breath. Then his lips came down on hers, and his arms went round her.

CHAPTER TEN

SARA was shaken and trembling when at last he released her. His eyes were very dark, almost gentle as he looked at her. 'Is that part of the job?' she whispered. 'Because I don't think——'

'No, it's not part of the job. I shouldn't kiss you—except in public. I shouldn't presume——'

'Then don't,' she whispered, 'please don't.'

'I won't, not any more.' He moved away, walked over towards the window. From there he turned to look at her. 'Not again.' And he went out. Sara looked at the empty space. That was it—easy; too easy. 'Don't.' 'I won't. Not any more.' Just like that. She should feel relieved. Her job would be so much easier with no added complications— why then did she feel a hollowness inside?

Sighing, she picked up her bag, found her lipstick and put some on, then went out the same way as Morgan had. They were going out for a pleasant ride, the four of them, destination unknown. And probably tomorrow, or the day after that, she would unofficially begin her very unofficial job of answering the telephone and smoothing the rough edges of Morgan's complicated life while at the same time being the happy, loved and loving fiancée. And if that's not complicated enough for me, she thought, as she walked to where Monique and Bernard were waiting, I have to go and fall hard for him, and because the last thing in the world I want is for him to find out, I have to go and act like an outraged virgin when he kisses me. Only it won't happen again——

'Hello!' called Monique. 'That's a lovely dress.' She herself wore cream slacks and matching silk over-blouse, and spiky-heeled gold sandals. She was elegant, chic, but seemingly without conceit.

'Thank you,' Sara sat beside her. 'I've got something to tell you later.'

'Oh! Interesting?' Monique waved her hand slightly, and Bernard, with a comical little shrug, wandered away, sighing. Both women laughed. 'Can you tell me now?'

'Briefly. I've agreed to stay on for a while as—wait for it— Morgan's social secretary. Basically it means protecting him from all the social invitations, and as I'm his official fiancée, they'll have to like it or lump it.'

'*I* like it,' Monique exclaimed, delighted. 'How pleasant— for me! That's selfish of me, I know, but you're so refreshing, Sara, so different from everyone else—I hope we'll see a lot of one another.'

'I hope so too.'

'Good. I occasionally go up to Paris for the weekend. I have a small apartment there, near Bernard's school. Would you like to come with me some time? I manage a few theatre visits, and shopping, of course——'

'Sounds fun.' Sara was about to add more, when Morgan appeared, dangling his car keys, and Monique raised her voice.

'Sara was just telling me the good news, Morgan. I'm so pleased. And she'll be able to visit Paris with me when I go, won't she?'

He looked at them both. 'If you wish, of course, Sara.'

'Oh, I do.'

'Are we ready?'

They both stood up, Morgan took Monique's arm, and Bernard skipped ahead. Sara walked behind. She was slightly puzzled. It could well have been her imagination, but somehow she doubted it. Morgan was not pleased at Monique's suggestion. She decided to ask Monique later, to see if she had noticed as well. But if she were right, a simple question remained. Why?

It was late evening. Monique and Bernard had both gone to bed, tired after a ride out that had taken them past Nice, and out for dinner to a quiet restaurant where they had, inevitably, met some friends of Morgan's. He knew everyone, everywhere, Sara was coming to the conclusion. He had told her that she was magnificent—that had been a prelude to his asking her to stay, a subtle piece of flattery that, allied with the rest, had worked only too well. He used her as he used everyone. She had no illusions about that, nor had she any about the part she played in his life. When her usefulness ceased, when his life was organised, she would go, and he would forget her quicker than yesterday's news.

She wondered if he would ever meet the woman who could capture his heart completely. It would take someone extra special. She would be beautiful, and she would have to have a charisma to match his. Not necessarily wealthy— Morgan had enough for anyone—but with a personality, a flair for living, a magnetism—Sara sighed, and gave a wry smile. She was standing by the pool, leaning on the low wall, looking out at the moonlit sea glittering in the distance. It was a warm night, the sky star-studded, the moon, a full one, high and pure and bright, remote. Sara had no illusions about herself. She considered herself very ordinary, fairly attractive—able, after the make-up session in Paris, to make the best of her features—intelligent—she found she was making a cool assessment of herself, and smiled wryly into the darkness. And why not? There was time. Morgan was in his study catching up on some paperwork. She had offered to help but been politely refused. He hadn't said she would find the work beyond her, and the implication had been slight, but it was there. So, who cares? she said defiantly, but not out loud.

She heard music coming from somewhere in the house— Martine and her husband, probably, watching television.

She was truly alone. Let's face it, she told herself, there's no hope you'll ever find him in love with you, so don't kid yourself. *But*—she put her finger to her lips and tapped thoughtfully, *but* you can make the most of your time here. Can I? she answered herself. Yes, you can! Oh, how? It was like talking to her alter ego. They'd take me away if I was saying this aloud, she said, inwardly. So what? You're not, the inner voice answered. True. She nodded. Let's have it, then. Right, why not work on a scheme for self-improvement while you're here? That sounds interesting, what does it mean? I'm glad you asked that question. She found she was mentally addressing a stone urn full of flowers, and giggled softly.

Well, think for a moment. I am, I am, her other self answered. Look around you, observe—watch, listen. There's Monique for a start. She's got chic, no doubt about it, and panache, and you get on extremely well, now you've got over that ridiculous jealousy—there's no need to drag that into it, her other self observed sternly. I apologise, thought Sara. So, okay, I'll ask Monique for lessons in panache—if it can be learned. *And* I'll go to a beauty salon and have the full works and study all I can about diet and exercise, and—yes? prompted the little voice. And—well, generally develop my personality. See? Sounds fair enough. It should help when you get back to the big world in London. Precisely. She nodded to herself.

She turned, mind made up—and gave a little scream. A dark shadow moved, came towards her, and she tensed for flight—then he spoke. 'Sorry, did I scare you? I wasn't creeping deliberately—I was just about to speak.'

Sara put a hand to her thudding heart. 'Oh. I thought you were working?'

'I was. I came out for air. Can't get the damned figures to balance—and I've got to the stage where I get a different total each time.'

Now was the moment to begin. The old Sara would

retort smartly: 'Oh, tough—but you've already implied I'm not quite bright enough to help, so don't except *me* to help you!'

The new Sara—the one with the beginnings of panache, and she really must look that up in the dictionary some time—said instead: 'Lead me to them. I'm quite good at figures, actually.' And she gave him a brilliant smile that unfortunately Morgan couldn't see.

'Would you?' He took her arm, led her past the pool along the terrace and across the dining room towards his study.

It was a large comfortable untidy room. He had already told her that this was his inner sanctum, and Martine was allowed in very briefly each week for cleaning. No one else. It showed. Papers and files overflowed on an overcrowded desk, and an ashtray half full of stubbed cheroots was evidence of his occupation. 'Sit down,' he said. 'Coffee?'

'Please.' He produced a coffee jug and poured her out a cup. Then he handed her a long sheet of paper; closely written columns of figures filled it.

'Oh. I'd better sit at the desk.' She moved towards it, eyes skimming down the page, handing him her cup to hold, and sat down, moved aside a pile of ledgers, laid the paper out before her, finger on top figures, looked up briefly. 'Pencil?' she enquired.

'Hmm—here.' He handed her one.

'I'll drink the coffee in a moment. Please don't talk,' she said, then she searched for and found a piece of scrap paper, and laid it beside the one she was studying. She took a deep breath, concentrated hard, and began the slow laborious process of adding the figures. The challenge was exhilarating, and her brain was clear and functioning in top gear.

She finished, wrote her result on the scrap paper, raised a hand as he appeared to be about to speak, and said: 'Hang on, I'm going to add up in reverse, just to double check. Haven't you ever heard of calculators?' She spared him a brief glance.

Silently he handed her one. 'I kept getting different answers with *that*,' he said with heavy irony.

'Dear me! You'd better check your batteries.' She switched it on and began tapping out numbers, all her concentration on the task. A minute or so later she wrote a figure down, switched the calculator off and looked at him. 'All done,' she said. She said it quietly, pleasantly, without the trace of a smirk. This is the new Sara, she told herself, remember?

Morgan took the scrap paper with its two identical results written neatly down. 'Amazing,' he said.

'Perhaps you were tired,' she said quite kindly. 'Is that all?' She drank her coffee with enjoyment.

'Thank you. Er—there is something else.'

'Okay.'

'Sure you don't mind?'

'Mind? No, of course not. I quite enjoy figures.'

He produced another, larger, longer sheet with more columns on it. 'I hadn't even started on that,' he admitted.

'Never mind. Perhaps you'd better sit down. This could take longer.' She put it flat out, turned the scrap paper over and began the laborious totting up again. Silence reigned. She was aware of him moving very quietly away, going out, the door closing, but she didn't falter. Steadily she went on, mind wonderfully sharpened with her success, totally concentrating on what she was doing.

When Morgan returned, she had written down her figures and was about to check with the calculator. She looked up as he came in. He was carrying a fresh pot of coffee and a plate of sandwiches. 'Want a break?' he asked. She stretched and flexed her fingers. 'I think so. Mmm, these look nice.' The bread was brown and crusty-looking. Sara peeped inside her sandwich; it contained rough paté and thinly sliced tomatoes. She had eaten scarcely anything all day.

'Martine's own paté. I made them myself. Hope the bread's not too thick for you.'

She bit into the bread. 'It's fine,' she managed after a few moments chewing. 'Just what I needed.'

'You're a wizard with figures,' commented Morgan, coming to stand behind her. 'Any other hidden talents?'

She smiled. 'I write a fair copperplate, but there's not a lot of demand for that nowadays.'

'Show me.' He put a piece of clean blank paper in front of her, and a fountain pen. Sara picked it up and wrote: 'The quick brown fox jumps over the lazy dog,' in bold and beautiful writing, and handed it to him.

'Don't ask. There are no more,' she said flippantly. But there are darned well going to be, she added inwardly.

'Very attractive. You're artistic, very artistic,' he said.

'Thank you. I do draw as well—quick sketches, you know.'

'I thought you said——'

'I don't count that.' She picked another piece of paper, looked at him steadily, added: 'Stand still,' and began to draw him. She worked quickly, having picked up both the talent and the method from her father, and in minutes it was done. She was pleased to see a fair likeness of him on the paper. She handed it to him. 'There you are.'

He gave a low whistle, then began to laugh. 'That is fantastic!' he said at last.

She smiled. 'Please—you'll make me blush, sir.' Flippant, casual, she surprised herself. My little pep talk did me good, she thought.

'I mean it. Mind you, I have that sketch your father did of mine. There's a great similarity of style, you know.' He shook his head. 'Amazing!'

'Dad used to do a lot of pictures like that, before he was

ill. He enjoyed them. I used to love watching him. Our local library has several of his paintings and sketches on exhibition in the reading room.' She stopped, memories flooding back, causing her a sweet pain. She had forgotten them. It was so long since she had been to the library, not since—She looked up and smiled. 'Well, I'd better get on with these sums.' She picked up the calculator, and it was blurred until she blinked hard a few times. Morgan went over to the window and stood looking out. The only sound in the room was the click of the calculator as her fingers registered the numbers.

'Done!' she said after several minutes. 'Phew!'

He turned round. 'It balances?'

She looked very levelly at him. 'Oh, yes.'

'Thank you very much.' He walked over to her. 'I appreciate your help.'

'You're welcome. Any more?'

'Not tonight. It's late.'

'But there is more?'

'There's always more,' he assured her.

'Then tomorrow, let me help.'

'That's not what you're here for.'

'I know.' She stood and leaned her hands on the desk. 'But I don't like doing nothing. Can I speak frankly, Morgan?'

He smiled slightly. 'You have to ask?'

'No, not really. It's this. I can't sit around doing nothing —my tasks as your "social secretary" will hardly be arduous, and while I love swimming and sunbathing and walking round the shops as much as anyone else, I'll get bored after a while—I need to be active. I'd be delighted to help in any aspect of your work—and don't worry, anything I see or hear will be strictly confidential. Do I make myself clear?'

'You always do, Sara.' He nodded. 'Obviously I've got staff, and accountants, but there are inevitably parts of my work that I and only I can co-ordinate—I'd appreciate your assistance.'

'You've got it.' She smoothed back her glossy cap of hair. 'Can we agree on hours?'

'You suit yourself.'

'No, I don't. I suit you. Obviously there are better days for you as far as this type of work goes than others. I only ask so that I can arrange my time accordingly. I might as well tell you now.' She hesitated. In for a penny, in for a pound. 'I've been thinking about things, and I've decided, I'm here for a while, and I know very well that putting on the act as your fiancée and doing the social bit aren't going to take up all my time, so I'm going to learn.'

'Learn what?'

'Everything!' She lifted her arms and raised her face ceilingwards, her face alight with the joy of her decision. Then she laughed at the look of sheer blank incomprehension on his face. 'Don't you *see*!' she exclaimed. 'I have a glorious opportunity to acquire chic while I'm here. Monique will help me, I know. And I'm going to study people—Oh I know you think they're all shallow and empty-headed, and I'm sure you're right—but that doesn't matter. There's a—a—polish, if you like, an air of confidence that I'm lacking in. I'm jolly well going to acquire it.' She stopped, seeing his face. 'You think I'm crazy, don't you?' she accused. 'I'm not, I'm very sane. You'll see—you won't know me when I leave.'

'Why should you want to change?'

'Tsk! Haven't you been listening?' She regarded him with amusement. 'Look, why did you buy me clothes, get my hair done—and the make-up?'

'To give you the confidence to carry off your new rôle.'

'Right! And I'm following it on, that's all. I'm going to go to a beauty parlour, have saunas, do exercises——'

'You *are* mad,' he said quietly.

Exasperated, she shook her head. 'I told you you'd think that——'

'You don't need to change.' His words shook her, but only for a moment. She smiled at him.

'Oh *no*,' she said with heavy sarcasm. 'Of course not. Little Miss Sara Bourne fits in beautifully.'

'No, you don't. You're individual. You're *different*.'

'I know damned well I am. No gloss, no—no panache.'

'A personality that's *yours*, not some product that's turned out of a mould like jelly,' he insisted.

'Hah! Easy for you to talk. I mean, look at you! You've got it all—style, panache, an air of self-confidence that could be quite insufferable if—if——' she floundered. 'Well, anyway, you *have*. And it's easy for you to tell me I'm an individual. Maybe—but what *kind*?'

'Don't you know?' he said.

'I wouldn't ask if I did, would I?' she retorted. 'It's what I'm going to find out over the next few days—or weeks— or months.' A silence fell as she finished speaking, and the words seemed to echo inside her head. Days—or weeks—or months. Months, months—would it be?

'Look in a mirror,' said Morgan quietly.

'I see my face when I do that.' She patted her cheek and touched her nose as she said, 'Two eyes, nose—yes, just one—a mouth. What on earth would you expect me to see?'

He shook his head, and she laughed. 'For heaven's sake! What do *you* see when you look in the mirror? The Hallé Orchestra?'

'Myself. I don't make a habit of it, though.'

'And I should? Is that it? All right.' She went over to a long mirror in an alcove by the window and studied her reflection, and as she did he came up behind her, and for a few moments, until she couldn't, for some reason, bear it any longer and turned away, she saw the two of them, he so incredibly dark and striking looking, she young—and afraid.

'No,' she whispered. 'It doesn't work.' But she had been shaken by that strange, brief moment of time when, standing together, she had seen them almost—blending; almost as one person, unmoving, still. It was time to move, to break the spell before it caught hold of her and she lost all semblance of reality. She looked up at Morgan, wanting him to take hold of her, to love her, to stay always there. 'It's late,' she said. 'I'm tired, I'm sorry. It was silly of me to tell you those things——' She gave a little laugh that didn't quite come off. 'You wouldn't understand.'

'Perhaps I do, better than you imagine—and perhaps I see more than you.'

'Well, you would. You've lived longer than I have.'

'Not because of that. It has nothing to do with years.'

'What then?' She wanted to move away. She couldn't. The spell wasn't broken at all. She was held in a fragile web and he had woven it around her, and she didn't know how to break free, and in a way she didn't want to.

'Soon you'll know.'

'You talk in riddles.' She was almost breathless. 'You're always talking in riddles—like telling me to see more and observe less. I never did understand what you meant. I suppose you think I'm rather dim—but then I'm not used to meeting people like you.' There was a sense, a feeling that went deeper than words, a dizzying spiral, a shifting of levels. She was no longer sure where she was, only he stood out in that room like a force she had never encountered before.

'Nor am I used to meeting people like you,' he echoed softly, and his words filled the room.

'Let me go,' she whispered.

'I'm not stopping you. I'm not touching you.'

'You are—not physically, but in a—a different way,' she said, and her eyes were wide, and she felt as if she had gone white.

'Then I am reaching you.'

'Yes—no—I don't know what you mean.' She turned her head as if seeking escape, and there was the door. She only had to walk towards it, but she couldn't.

They were standing only a foot or so apart. Morgan reached out to touch her cheek. His hand was warm. 'You know,' he said, 'that something began on that day I walked into your life, and something changed. There can be no going back. I came into your life because of a letter—an echo from the past—and I came at the right moment, when you despaired of what had happened to you, and were escaping from it. I could have come an hour later, and might never have found you, or a day earlier when everything would have seemed all right, and I might have gone away again—only I didn't. I arrived then, as you were on the point of leaving, and everything fell into place, and everything afterwards was as inevitable as night following day.' His hand, the hand that touched her cheek, was very gentle, gentle and strong. She made no attempt to take it away, or to move. She had to listen to his words because listening to him was the only thing she ever wanted to listen to, and his power was such that she felt as if she were caught up in it, and she loved him more than life itself, and she had never known what love was, before this moment, this now that was lasting for ever.

'Yes,' she said. 'Oh, yes.' She sighed. 'I know.'

'I think you're beginning to, anyway.' He put his other hand on her shoulder. 'Look at me.'

She gazed into his eyes, seeing the tiny reflections of herself in them, and he smiled slowly. 'You don't need to change,' he said.

'No,' she whispered. 'No.' She felt dizzy, and the room started to spin round and she clutched his hand, frightened. 'Hold me—I feel—faint,' she said, and as she did, a roaring, rushing sound filled her head. The last thing she saw, as the grey mist filled her, was his face, and the last thing she felt were his arms going round her, and she heard, distantly through the waterfall of sound, his voice, saying her name.

CHAPTER ELEVEN

SHE was lying on her bed, and Morgan was holding a damp towel and smoothing it over her forehead and burning cheeks. She opened her eyes and saw him, felt the cold trickle of water on her face, and said:

'What happened?'

'You passed out. Stay still, you'll be all right. Sara, you ate hardly anything today, did you?'

'I had a sandwich——' It was coming back to her now. They had been in his study, talking, and then everything had gone blank.

'And that was about all. You picked at your lunch, you picked at your dinner tonight——'

'Don't lecture me, please,' she said faintly.

Morgan gave a half smile, half grin. 'Sorry. Want anything?'

'No—a drop of brandy? Would that be all right?'

'Yes. Stay there, don't *move*.'

He went out very quietly and Sara, disobeying, crept to the bathroom. She saw her white face in the mirror before she crept back again, and just made it before he came in with a brandy glass.

'Thanks.' She sipped. It was a smooth cognac, and it warmed her instantly. She lay back after drinking a small portion of it. 'I'll be all right now,' she said.

'I'm not leaving you yet. I should have kept the nurse on. She could have had a look at you.' His face was very serious.

She managed a weak smile. 'There's nothing wrong with me,' she said. 'Honestly.' Morgan put his hand on her forehead. She felt as if it were burning.

'Too much sun—too little food——'

154

'Yes, doctor,' she said.

'You little fool! And you let me give you those figures to do.'

'I volunteered, didn't I?' She turned her head slightly away.

'I shouldn't have let you.'

It wasn't the figures, it was what happened afterwards, she wanted to say, but didn't. And in any case, there was another reason for her stupid faint, but one she could hardly tell him either. He'd think she was too delicate for words. . . .

'For heaven's sake, it was nothing,' she protested. 'Really.' She sat up, and regretted it instantly. He caught hold of her.

'Steady! You're as white as a——'

She bit her lip. 'I'll be all right in a——'

'No, dammit, you won't.' He laid her back and stood up. 'I'm going to phone the doctor.'

'No!' She leaned over and caught his arm. 'Please—no—it's not necessary.' He sat down on the bed and took her hand gently off his arm. 'Look, I *know* what's the matter with me, and I don't need a doctor—you wouldn't under-stand——' She gave him a glance that was a combination of exasperation and embarrassment. 'There's nothing a doctor can do.'

'Ah!' Understanding dawned, and he gave a wry smile. 'Sorry.'

'Don't keep apologising,' she said fiercely. 'I overdid the sun, and the swimming—my own fault, I should have realised.' She pulled a face. 'And please don't think I'm ill, because I'm not—but I'd appreciate a hot drink. Not coffee.'

'Hot chocolate?'

'Mmm, sounds fine.'

'And two aspirins?'

'I dare say I could force them down too if you insist.'

'I'll be right back. Look, get ready for bed, okay? I want

to see you settled.' Morgan stood up and looked at her. 'You're quite safe——' And he was gone. Sara stifled an unwilling smile, then, grabbing her nightie, she went into the bathroom to undress.

When he returned she was sitting up in bed demurely clad in her old cotton dressing gown over her new nightdress. He tapped on the door and waited until she called: 'Come in,' before entering. He carried two steaming beakers.

'Mind if I join you?' he asked.

'Do you *like* drinking chocolate?'

'Why not? It makes a change.' He handed her one, and two aspirins.

She laughed. It was different, so very different now. The conversation in his study had been so deep and profound, stripping raw all emotions, getting to the heart of everything, a strange, disturbing time—and now he was different, so completely changed that it was like being with a different man. She loved this one as well. She loved him so very much that it hurt.

'Mmm, this is gorgeous.' She sipped the hot creamy chocolate with appreciation. 'I feel better already.' But she didn't, not really.

'I try to give satisfaction.'

'I'm sure you do.' She had propped up her pillows, and sat back comfortably.

'You had me worried before, when you passed out,' he told her.

'Did I? I'm sorry. It's never happened before—just a combination of things, I suppose. I don't make a habit of it, I promise you.' She looked into her beaker.

'And you're sure you're all right?'

'Really. Did you mean what you said before, about not wanting me to change?'

'Yes.'

'Does than mean—you don't want me to go to the places with Monique?' she asked.

'If you want to, of course you must. Just don't get too influenced by them, that's all. Stay—yourself.'

'And when she mentioned Paris. Why don't you want me to go there?'

'Did I say I didn't?' asked Morgan

'No, but I saw your face. It was enough.'

'We'll talk about it later—tomorrow,' he said. 'It's gone midnight.'

'Why not now?'

'Because.'

'That's no reason,' Sara protested.

'No, but it's all you're getting. Drink up. I'm going to see you settled in bed and asleep before I go.'

She grinned. 'I'd have a job to sleep with you here!'

'I don't think so,' he answered.

'You sound very sure.'

'I am. Those were two sedative pills I gave you. The doctor left them for Monique. They'll knock you out.'

'You had no right——' she began, and looked suspiciously at her drink, then at him.

'It's all right, I didn't drug that as well. And they won't hurt you. They're just strong tranquillisers, that's all. I thought they'd help you relax.'

'I'm perfectly relaxed now.' It was true. She felt very drowsy.

He grinned. 'They're working.'

'You should have told me——' she said. Her words were getting blurred.

'Would you have taken them if I had?'

'No.'

'Well then, I did you a good turn.' Morgan reached out to take the beaker from her. 'Careful!'

Sara lay back and yawned. 'Oh, I'm tired.'

'I can see that.' He took one pillow away. 'Lie down.'

'Hold my hand,' she said, and held hers out. 'Don't go yet——' She stopped. It seemed she was saying things that she ought not to, but it also seemed quite all right. What had he said? That she was safe? She yawned again, and felt his strong fingers curl over hers; mmm, that was *nice*. She closed her eyes and her head felt delightfully floaty, as if it might float away....

'I won't leave you yet,' she heard him say, as if from a great distance, and they were the nicest words she had ever heard. Then she was asleep.

When she awoke it was the middle of the night and her room was a greyish blur, and she was still drowsy, but something had roused her from a deep confused dream. She turned in bed, and Morgan lay asleep beside her, on top of the covers. He was dead to the world, and his arm was across her, and there were no covers over him. She felt a warm surge of love for him, leaned up and pulled the spread from her side, and covered him with it. He made not a move or a sound. Sara sighed, snuggled against him, and fell asleep again.

When next she awoke, it was morning. She turned her head on the pillow to look at the sleeping man beside her. The cover she had pulled over him had partly fallen off. She laid it very carefully and slowly over him. She didn't want him to wake yet, not yet. She had never shared a bed with a man before. She wondered if he had ever shared a bed with a woman without making love to her.

The last thing she remembered was asking him to hold her hand. Had he sensed her unspoken need? She gazed steadily at his sleeping face. In repose he looked gentle, younger. Not soft, just—gentle. She remembered their arrival at the children's home, and how two youngsters had rushed up to him tugging at him, and he had swung them up in his arms and carried them, laughing, in with him. She remembered how he was with Bernard. Tough and hard he might be, but as in all truly strong men there was a gentle side. He was himself at all times, no need to prove anything to anybody. She breathed a sigh, her eyes lingering on his face, caressing every line of it, the high cheek-bones, deep-set eyes, dark brows, mouth faintly curved in a half smile, as if his dream was a pleasant one. She wanted to touch his mouth, run her finger down his cheek to trace the softened outline, to touch the roughness of his beard growth, the dark shadow that was evidence of his virility—touch the faint pulse at his throat—she swallowed. Her throat hurt with the pain of suppressed tears. She wanted to weep.

He had stayed with her because she had needed him, and hadn't been well, and it couldn't have been very comfortable for him, lying on top of the covers, with not much space, and she wished he were in the bed with her, and could have held her close all night.

Morgan stirred, mumbled something, and tried to turn over, then he opened his eyes, and looked at her. It was clear that he wasn't sure where he was. 'Um?' he said; his eyes were blank.

Sara laughed softly. 'It's all right, you're safe.'

Then he knew. 'Good God,' he said, with feeling. 'Have I been here all night?'

'I'm afraid so.' She sat up, and so did he, pulling the cover off him and swinging his legs down to sit at the side, where he put his hands to his head, rubbed it vigorously, and yawned.

'Oh,' he groaned, 'I ache all over.'

'I'm not surprised. You had about one foot of space—stay there, I'll go and get you a cup of coffee.' Sara pulled back the covers. 'Get in and have five minutes of comfort. I'll not be long.'

It was seven. With any luck, Martine would have gone to market, as she did every day except Sunday. And if she hadn't, Sara would get one cup of coffee and pretend it was for her.

The kitchen was empty. She made two cups, very hot, and when she returned with them Morgan was fast asleep in her bed. He looked much more comfortable. Sara put the coffee down and went to the bathroom. Minutes later, after a brief but refreshing shower, she went back to see him snoring gently on his back.

She slipped inside the bed, careful not to disturb him, and sipped her coffee, which was far too hot, so she lay down beside him. She wouldn't sleep, but she was going to stay with him until he woke, and it was time for him to go. She was pleasantly drowsy, and nothing could spoil this time, and it would certainly never happen again. She knew she was being foolish. She should have sent him back to his own bed when he had woken minutes before. She knew what she should have done, but she had no intention of doing it.

She snuggled down beside him and allowed herself the luxury of fantasy, of this being their room, their own place, safe from the world, a haven, a shelter of love, a place where she could be in his arms. . . .

Her heart, her mind, her body, were filled with the blazing wonder of her love for him. Nothing would ever be the same again, after this. She would probably meet a man, one day, whom she would love, and be happy with, and whose children she would bear, but nothing would ever take this time from her, and when she was old she would remember, and her heart would go warm again with the memories of a love so perfect, perhaps more perfect for lasting such a brief time, like a bright golden dream that could be recaptured at will.

The sun flooded into the room, slanting golden rays as if to confirm her thoughts. She looked round her, seeing everything with fresh eyes, to imprint it on her mind, to encapsulate it for ever and ever. . . .

Oh, Morgan, if you knew how I loved you, she thought, but you never will, for all the women fall for you, and make it obvious with blatant pursuit, and if I did that it would be spoiled—it would be just like the rest you seek to escape. How ironic, she thought. I'm the one to protect *you* from the others, and I love you more than they do; yet it's one thing I can do for you.

She would stay at the villa, until she sensed it was time for her to leave. She wouldn't wait until he wanted her to go—she would know when her job was done, then she would slip quietly away, back to England, so that he wouldn't have the embarrassment of telling an unwanted guest to leave. She would know. She knew so much about him, deep inside her, and when the time came she wouldn't look back. She would live her life to the full, with no regrets. Because she was not of his world, nor he of hers, that grew more obvious each day. He was wealthy beyond anything she had ever known. Wealthy with money that his father had had left to him, and handed down to his son, and Morgan, equally clever, had increased it beyond her comprehension. The figures she had added up had been in millions of francs—the turnover for the hotel, and restaurants, and a few shops. She smiled wryly. Any one of those shops took in more in a month than her uncle made in a year, and Morgan hadn't even mentioned them to her. He hadn't even remembered. Monique had told her, casually expecting her to know, and been only mildly surprised that Sara didn't.

She had laughed when Sara had confessed her ignorance. 'He has a finger in so many pies,' she had said. 'I don't think he knows what he is worth—and sometimes one senses that he would give it all up tomorrow if he could.'

No wonder it meant nothing to him to yield his shares in the restaurants he and Jack owned. The mill was more important. The mill, for people from whom he could expect no financial gain, only the satisfaction of lives, young lives, helped. Monique didn't know about the children's home. No one did, except Sara herself. She wondered why he had told her. She would probably never know. That, too was something to remember . . . .

Morgan put his arm round her and pulled her to him, and snuggled his head against her neck. 'That's better,' he said drowsily. 'Much more comfortable. I shouldn't be here——'

'I know you shouldn't. And your coffee's cold,' she whispered. Her heart was beating fast.

'Mmm, is it? Damn the coffee anyway. I've got to get up soon—tell me I've got to stay here.'

'You've got to stay here,' she repeated obediently.

'All right.' He closed his eyes. He was asleep. Sara lay there in the warmth of his arms, and it *was* right. It was the rightest thing ever. If I could choose a moment for time to stand still, it would be now, she thought, and closed her eyes.

She awoke to find herself being kissed. It was a very tender kiss, and she opened her eyes and slid her hand round Morgan's neck, and responded, with the memory of a delightful dream she had just had still clearly in her mind.

For minutes they lay there together, clinging to each other, no words spoken, for none were needed, until at last he whispered huskily: 'Time for me to go,' and she said:

'I know.'

His eyes looked deep into hers, only inches away, too close to focus properly, a lovely blur, and she saw the smile in them. 'You're quite safe—very safe,' he murmured, 'but I'm not so sure about myself. Tell me I've got to go now.'

'No,' she mouthed.

'You're a wicked temptress,' he groaned.

'I know.' She moved her head forward just that inch or two needed, and found his mouth, ever so gently, teasing it with her tongue before she put her lips to his. It was a deep, satisfying kiss that lasted for ever and it was Sara who moved away first, her heart pounding. 'Perhaps you better had,' she whispered. He slid his warm hand lazily up her arm, subtly caressing it with featherlight fingers until he reached her neck.

'Want to know why you're wicked?' he asked.

'No.'

'Well, I'll tell you,' he ran his finger round her ear, gently, wonderingly, as if he had never seen one before. 'It's because I would be making love to you now—and you know it—and this is hell for me because you also know damned well I can't, and won't, and you don't care, do you?'

'No,' she whispered, and gave a low throaty chuckle that he silenced most effectively with another, even more deliciously heart-stopping kiss.

She slid her arm round his waist, the soft silkiness of his shirt warm to her hand. Then up his back to his shoulder blades, where she massaged gently and instinctively.

'Is that better?' she murmured, when at last she could speak.

'Should it be?'

'I thought it might help—you did say you ached all over.'

'I don't ache in that way—not any more.'

'Oh. How then?'

'Oh God——' he buried his face in her hair. 'Do I have to tell you?'

'No, I don't think so.' She could scarcely breathe with the heady sense of love that filled her. Warm, tingling, sensual—she was mad, and so was he, and neither seemed capable of doing anything about it. She felt the tremor of him against her. He was controlled, but only just. It was true, what he said. He would have made love to her—she knew a sense of power over him, and she stroked his black black hair gently, then his roughened cheek.

'My face will be raw,' she whispered. 'You need a shave.'

'Serve you right.' He pulled her to him and rubbed his cheek against hers and she squealed in protest and pushed him away. 'Ouch, that hurt, you brute!'

'It's the least I can do. Give me some satisfaction——'
he stopped, touched her cheek, which burned. 'Sorry——'
and kissed it. 'That better?'

'No. You're a beast——' she ran her fingers up his
ribs and he collapsed against her.

'Don't—stop—Sara, please——' he was trying to stifle
anguished laughter. She did it all the more and he reached
to her hand and pulled it away. 'Don't do that,' he grated.

'You're ticklish!' she giggled.

'So? Are you?'

'I don't know—no—please, Morgan, don't——' she
pleaded—and he stopped immediately and his eyes had
gone very dark, almost black. He looked at her, and then
they weren't laughing any more, the joke was over, and
she saw the pain in his eyes, the torture, and they were both
trembling, and he murmured brokenly:

'Oh God, Sara, send me away.'

Sobbing, the tears she could no longer stop welling
out and down her cheeks, she clung to him. 'I'm sorry,'
she said. 'I'm sorry——'

'Don't cry, please don't cry.' Morgan's voice was hushed,
shaking with emotion. He held her tightly against him,
held her to him and kissed her closed eyes as she shivered
uncontrollably in his arms. 'I can't leave you like this—oh,
my dear, please stop.' But she couldn't, and he cradled
her to him, comforting her, holding her like the baby she
knew she was, and the passion melted into warmth, glowing
warmth that filled them both, and filled the room, and
gradually the sobs died down to a murmur and she said:

'It's all right—it's all right. I'm sorry I was—stupid.'

He sat up slightly and looked down at her, and wiped a
last tear away. 'Sure?'

She nodded. 'Yes. You'd better go now.' He closed his
eyes for a moment or two, then took hold of her hand and
kissed the palm.

'Yes, I better had.' He slid out of bed, then bent to kiss her cheek. 'You're to stay there for a while. I'll send Martine in with your beakfast.' As she was about to protest, he added: 'That's an order.'

He picked up his shoes and went towards the window. He turned and looked back at her briefly, his face serious, not smiling, then he went out.

Sara lay back. She couldn't think coherently, she didn't want to think, she just wanted to lie there. Everything was too close. Her head whirled, her body burned as though with a fever. She felt totally exhausted, yet at the same time filled with a kind of exhilaration. Nothing could ever be the same again. She closed her eyes and the images and sensations whirled about in her brain, sharply coloured, beautiful. She felt as if she could float away at any moment. . . .

CHAPTER TWELVE

'WHY don't we drive over to my home?' said Monique. 'I must fetch some more clothes.'

'All right,' Sara agreed. Bernard had been taken to visit a friend of his who was at home recovering from measles, and the two women sat comfortably on the terrace after having eaten a salad lunch. Neither was hungry, and Morgan, who had gone out before Sara got up, had telephoned to say he would be out all day.

Monique was staying for two or three more days at Morgan's invitation, and Bernard was to return to school the following evening. The two women had spent a pleasant hour talking, and Sara had told her some of her ideas for self-improvement, which had caused Monique to laugh merrily and echo, practically word for word, Morgan's own reaction. 'Why bother?' she had said. 'You are fine as you are.' Sara had explained briefly and as best she could, why, and Monique had nodded thoughtfully.

'As you wish, of course,' she had said.

They resumed the conversation now, as Jacques, Martine's husband, drove them in the Mercedes to where Monique lived. 'Any advice I can give you about clothes,' she said, 'I will be only too happy to do. I love buying clothes—as you will gather when you see my wardrobe! We are much of a size, Sara—you must try some on, and we'll get an idea that way of what suits you.'

'It sounds fun,' Sara smiled at her.

'Oh, it is.' She sighed. 'I'm glad you're staying for a while. I feel as if we've known each other a long time.' She looked at Sara. 'Nearly there.' They were approaching a white-walled garden, very large, and in the distance, higher up, could be seen a beautiful house. Jacques turned in the gateway and they went up a drive surrounded by old trees and flowering bushes. The house was large, three-storied, with arched windows on the ground floor, and a balcony of wrought iron above that running practically the length of the house. Huge elms dominated the front of the drive, Jacques stopped gently in front of the wide Palladian style entrance.

'Thank you, Jacques,' Monique spoke in French. 'We will ring when we need you.'

'Oui, madame. Au revoir.' He was a man of few words, not surly, but self-contained, a contrast to his talkative wife. They watched him drive away and then went inside.

'A drink first, then we'll look round.' Monique raised her voice. 'Hortense, c'est moi!'

A plump woman bustled out from somewhere at the back of the house and greeted them, enquiring after Madame's health, being assured that Madame was much better but was staying away a couple more days and needed some clothes, but first a drink.

Hortense bustled away and Monique led Sara into an exquisite room furnished in shades of cool lime green. It overlooked a patio and swimming pool. Monique flung down her bag and kicked off her shoes. 'Make yourself comfortable,' she said. She sat down on a settee. 'Ah, that's better. Tell me more, Sara. You're going to be helping Morgan with his work?'

'Yes. But it won't occupy all my time. I just want to——' she shrugged, 'improve myself generally, acquire a bit of polish.'

Monique smiled, and when Hortense had been and gone, leaving two tall glasses and a jug of iced orange and a bottle of wine on a small table, said: 'There's no harm in that. Don't forget though that you are young, and nothing, but nothing, gives you greater advantage. However, with added confidence——' she laughed charmingly, 'who knows? The world will be yours.'

Sara grinned. 'I'm not asking for the world!'

'I know. I suspect—forgive me if I'm wrong—that you are already more than a little in love with Morgan, no?'

Sara felt herself grow pale. 'Is it so obvious?'

'No, it is not obvious at all—and certainly not to him. Men are remarkably unobservant, I have found—but it is to me.' Monique smiled. 'I can speak frankly because I am old enough to be your mother——'

'You can't be!' Sara cut in. 'I'm nineteen. I'll be twenty —oh, good heavens, I'd forgotten! It's my birthday this Saturday!' They both burst out laughing.

'Truly? My dear, we must get Morgan to arrange a party for you. Even at your ripe old age of twenty, I'm still old enough. I am forty-five.'

'I don't believe you,' Sara gasped. Monique looked thirty-five at most.

'Thank you, but it is true. So you see, the privilege of age gives me the right to speak freely to you—and I can see what others might not. You too have fallen under Morgan's spell—and living at the villa, and working with him as you do, and particularly playing the part of his fiancée—oh, la! c'est difficile, ça!'

'I know that,' Sara agreed. 'Why do you think I want to be more sophisticated?'

'So that he might fall for you?' Monique said shrewdly.

'I suppose, if I'm perfectly honest, yes,' Sara sighed. She looked across as Monique poured out the drinks. 'Go on, tell me I'm mad. He already has.'

'No, I don't think you are at all. I think you are a very clever girl, very wise——' you wouldn't have said that if you'd seen me this morning, thought Sara. 'And I can tell you this,' Monique handed Sara a glass. 'He is intrigued with you. I have seen—sometimes—the way he looks at you.'

Sara stared at her. If she was teasing, it was cruel—but Monique wasn't a cruel woman. Monique raised her glass. "No, I do not joke.'

Sara felt a shiver down her spine. She was a novelty to him, that was all. If he was intrigued it was because she was so young, and naïve. She shook her head. 'I'd like to believe that,' she said quietly, 'but——'

'*C'est vrai.* I know.' Monique gave her an impish smile. 'See, we will make our plans for Saturday, we will talk, this week, and who knows?'

Sara laughed. 'You cheer me up no end,' she said.

'Come, let us take our glasses and go and see what I have. I have forgotten myself what there is in my wardrobe. But we shall see, hey?'

The next hour or so was a revelation to Sara. Monique had a room upstairs with a long wardrobe running the entire length of one wall. It was like an Aladdin's cave, a treasure trove. Dress after dress was brought out for inspection, tried on, put aside for yet another. Every available surface was draped with dresses and skirts when at last Monique produced one with a flourish, and said: 'Now look at *this.*'

Sara looked. She had never seen anything so beautiful in her life. Monique was holding, at arm's length, a long floor-sweeping confection in swirly chiffon, shading from rich soft blue at the rounded neck to a sea green at the hem. The sleeves were long and full, and the effect was stunning. She went forward to touch it, and the chiffon was so fine it seemed almost too delicate to handle.

'Try this on. I have had it so long that I had almost forgotten it,' said Monique, and slipped it from the hanger. 'See, there is a slim-fitting full-length petticoat underneath.' The petticoat, in silk, was indeed slim-fitting. Sara sucked in her stomach instinctively and Monique chuckled. 'It will fit. Slip off your own waist slip.'

Sara did so and put the dress over her head, and

Monique zipped it up. 'Now the *pièce de résistance*,' she said. She lowered the outer dress gently over Sara's head, and Sara smoothed it down.

'Now, look in the mirror,' said Monique softly.

Sara walked to the mirror, and the chiffon swirled round her and the silken sheath underneath swished and swished as she moved. She stood and looked at herself, then raised her arms slightly from her side to get the full effect of the tapering full sleeves. 'Oh,' she said. It was all she was capable of saying. The low rounded neckline revealed the swell of her bosom and the dress swept away down to the floor, and she looked, and felt, like a medieval princess. It was perfect.

'It's simply beautiful,' she whispered.

'And it is yours,' Monique answered. 'And you will wear it at your birthday party.'

'Monique, thank you very much! I'll borrow it if I may, but I couldn't——'

'Nonsense! I have had it at least fifteen years. It is far too young for me now! But for you, it is quite perfect. I insist you accept it as a gift.'

'It's—I've never seen anything like it in my life!'

'It's a Dior original, my dear. There's only one dress like that in the world—and you are wearing it.' Monique bent to check the hem, spreading the soft folds wide. 'No, nothing needs altering. Take it with my blessing.'

'I don't know how to thank you,' Sara gasped. She twirled slightly, looking at it from every possible angle.

'You already have. Get changed while I go and find something to wear. Hortense will put these away and pack that up for you.'

Sara took it off carefully, and folded it up. Then she put her dress back on and went down to wait for Monique.

On Tuesday, Morgan took Sara to Louise and Jack's house for dinner. She was tempted to wear the beautiful dress that Monique had given her, but resisted. The parcel of dresses had arrived that morning from Paris, and she wore a simple black sheath dress with a softly shaped top in guipure lace. Morgan looked at her as she stepped into his car. 'You're sure you're up to it?' he asked.

'Of course.' He closed her door and went round to his side. 'I won't let you down—don't worry,' she said as he got in.

He had treated her, since Monday morning, as though she were made of glass. Not remote—not exactly, but—different. It seemed as if their closeness, that incredible warmth and loving, had ended something. He was different—even Monique had remarked on it that day to her, but there was nothing Sara could do about it. She had done some more work for him, earlier that day in his study, and he scrupulously avoided any personal contact. He was like a stranger. He was like one now. He drove along the road that led to Jack's house, and he seemed preoccupied. Perhaps it was because of what was to happen. It might, she thought unhappily, have been better if they hadn't spent the night together. Yet in an odd way it only made her more determined to succeed in what she had to do with Louise. She began to breathe deeply and calmly, relaxing her body, and as they neared the brightly lit villa where she was to meet Louise on her own home ground she looked calmly at him. 'You'll start the ball rolling?' she asked.

'I will.' He spared her a brief glance. 'After I've invited them to your birthday party on Saturday.'

'Right.'

'Why didn't you tell me?' he asked.

'About my birthday? I'd forgotten. It was only when Monique and I were talking about ages that it struck me.'

'It might be tactful not to mention that Monique is staying with us.'

'Of course I won't.'

And that was the end of their conversation. Sara mentally

braced herself as he turned into the driveway. This is it, she thought. My bit to help the children. It helped to crystallise her thoughts wonderfully.

The evening exceeded her own expectations. She felt as though she were walking a tightrope from the minute they were greeted by Louise, who looked stunning in red, to the moment they said their goodnights. She collapsed back into the comfort of the seat as they went down the drive. 'Oh God,' she sighed, 'I feel as though I've been through a wringer!'

'But you did it. You *did* it!' Morgan put his hand on her knee. It was an almost impersonal gesture, nothing faintly sexual in it at all. 'She swallowed the bait whole. I'm seeing Jack tomorrow—we spoke briefly when she took you to the bathroom. A slight push in the right direction—the land's as good as mine.' He laughed softly, took his hand away again to steer the car round a tricky bend, and Sara fell silent. This, originally, had been the sole purpose of her coming. Only now it had changed, so very much that the conquest of Louise seemed a minor matter. She was committed to so many other things, until the time came when she was no longer needed. . . .

She closed her eyes, tired, and was not aware that he looked at her, or the expression on his face. She was aware only of a hollow, empty feeling inside her.

Wednesday and Thursday passed in a blur of arrangements for the party. Monique had stayed on to help Sara, and was going to remain until Sunday, after the party was over. Sara, unused to such planning on a grand scale, was grateful to her and told her so. There were dozens of phone calls to be made, and Monique took charge of these. She, like Morgan, knew everybody, but even Sara had a shock when Monique told her the number of guests there would be.

'A hundred and fifty!' she gasped, as she took in a

drink to the woman sitting by the phone, list on the table before her.

'Morgan does things in style—besides, what better opportunity to introduce his fiancée to everyone?'

Sara sat down beside her. Morgan had gone to meet Jack in Cannes—and she knew why, It was mid-afternoon, Thursday, and she looked at the clock, wondering when he would return. It could be all over by now. He had met Jack the previous day, and had told her that all was well. There had been little opportunity to say more. Monique was there, and knew virtually nothing of the plans—and Morgan seemed to be making a point of avoiding seeing Sara alone. She felt puzzled by his aloofness—although it wasn't as obvious as that. It was as though—as though their relationship had changed subtly. He was up early every morning and away in his car immediately after breakfast, not returning until dinner, sometimes not even then.

She heard a car, then a door slam. 'That might be him now,' she said, and went outside, to see Jack getting out of his Rolls-Royce. She walked along the terrace to greet him. 'Hello. Isn't Morgan with you?' she said.

He looked up and grinned. 'I thought he'd be here by now,' he answered, bounding up the steps on to the terrace. 'I left him ages ago.'

'Let me get you a drink. Perhaps he's been held up somewhere.'

'Thanks——' he stopped. Monique was emerging from the dining room, cool and beautiful.

'Hello, Jack,' she said. 'What a pleasant surprise.' She went forward to shake his hand, the traditional greeting, and he answered:

'I didn't know you were still here, Monique. It's good to see you. You're looking very well.'

'Thank you.'

Sara murmured: 'I'll go and get the drinks,' and left. They didn't seem to have heard. She took her time in the kitchen, pausing to chat to Martine, then went back. Jack and Monique were sitting on the terrace talking. She put the bottle of wine and glasses down, said: 'Excuse me, I have to make a phone call,' and left them. She might not have spoken for all the notice they took of her.

She went quietly to the library and waited at the window. From there she could see the driveway. If Morgan arrived she intended to delay him. She might even be able to speak to him herself for a moment. Jack thought he should be back by now, so where was he? She waited, and after half an hour, when it would surely be unusual if she didn't return to the guests, she went back to the terrace. She knew immediately that something very serious had happened. Jack looked like a man in shock—and Monique had been crying. She had told him the truth about Bernard; Sara knew it could only be that.

'Do you want me to leave you?' she said quietly, and Monique shook her head.

'No, please—stay.' Jack looked at Sara. He looked as though he needed a drink.

'Coffee?' she suggested. 'Or brandy?'

'Coffee, please. Black.' He looked across the table where they sat, to Monique.

'Why didn't you tell me before?' he asked.

Monique said softly: 'Because you love Louise. How could I? It is only because you—spoke about Bernard—as if you—guessed, that I——' she stopped.

'Oh God!' Jack put his hand on the table so hard that the knuckles were white. 'I looked at him at lunch, and thought, how wonderful it would be to have a son like that. I thought, Louise refuses to have a child——' his voice broke. 'You say I love Louise. I—I loved her—once. I found out about her—lovers last year, and I forgave her—but she's made my life hell——'

'Please,' Monique laid her hand over Jack's, 'don't torture yourself.'

'All this time wasted,' he said, anguished. 'All this time—and *my* son!'

Sara melted away like a shadow. They didn't see her go. They didn't need her either. She had no part in what was happening between them. She wondered if Morgan's invitation to lunch, for her and Bernard, had been premeditated. If so it had been cleverly done. It had all seemed so accidental, the meeting with Jack, his return afterwards. She smiled to herself as she made a leisurely way to the kitchen. The coffee could wait; they had ten years to catch up on. She knew now why Morgan hadn't returned, when Jack had expected him to be there. At least she thought she knew, but she was wrong. How wrong, she didn't find out until the following day.

Four women cleaners from the nearby village arrived on Friday morning to prepare the villa for the party. Jacques and Marc were busy in the garden setting out fairylights, and Morgan left immediately after they had all breakfasted, saying he would be away until the afternoon.

Monique and Sara had a leisurely swim to keep out of the way of everyone, and sat afterwards by the pool talking. Monique told her everything that had happened since the previous day. She had gone out with Jack after Morgan had returned home.

'We went for dinner at a quiet little restaurant we used to go to many years ago,' she said. 'He has never taken Louise there.' She smiled sadly at Sara. 'I vowed I would never damage his marriage. It turns out that there is no real marriage to damage—and in a sense, you are responsible for that.'

'Me?' Sara looked at her, horrified.

'Don't look so worried! I should phrase it more tactfully. Since—you arrived, and Louise thought that you and Morgan are engaged, she has been hell to live with. Hysterical, even violent to him—he knew then that it was no good. He had tried for so long—but realising her feelings for Morgan——' she shrugged. 'And then meeting Bernard—and me—again,' she looked at Sara—'it made him see the truth. I have loved him for a long time, Sara. I was very foolish ten years ago, when I left him after a stupid quarrel —but I was a good wife to my husband, and I loved him too, in a way. I never forgot Jack, though. I never could, seeing Bernard growing——' she faltered. 'He is going to divorce Louise. And then, soon, we will be married.'

'I'm very happy for you, Monique,' said Sara softly.

'Thank you. You will understand why neither of them will be coming to the party tomorrow?'

'It seems best,' she agreed wryly.

'He has told me of the land Morgan wanted,' said Monique. 'That is safe. He has had Louise sign it over to him yesterday in return for all her gambling debts which he has now paid off. But now that he and Louise will not be staying married, he wants very much to keep in partnership with him.'

'It seems sensible. Why not?' He only wanted the piece of land, and the mill. He hadn't really wanted to break with Jack, Sara knew. It was all working out for the best.

'He is telling Louise today,' said Monique, 'then he's coming over here.'

'Oh, God!'

Monique sighed. 'It will not be—pleasant.'

'No. When he comes, I'll stay out of your way. You'll want to talk.'

'You mustn't! This is your home——'

Sara laughed. 'It isn't. I'm a guest too, remember?' She said it lightly. 'And anyway, I want to go into Cannes and do a bit of shopping. I'll phone for a taxi. Jacques is too busy to take me.'

'Will you come to the hairdressers with me tomorrow? For your party? I go to a marvellous place.'

'Why not? Sounds a good idea.'

They discussed the details of the catering that Morgan had arranged, and it seemed as if it were going to be a magnificent party. But all the time they talked, Sara had a nagging feeling of vague unhappiness. It wasn't her imagination. Morgan had been abstracted, impersonal, all week. Ever since Sunday night....

Even on the brief occasions that they had been alone—and those were rare, he was like a stranger, polite, courteous—she had done some more work for him the previous evening and he had treated her like a secretary. That was what she was, she thought ironically. He hadn't once touched her or even gone near her. And how could she ask him what was wrong? Because nothing was wrong. The laughter they had shared so briefly, during that long evening, and night, was gone, apparently for good. It was too amorphous even to explain to Monique—and in any case, she was too full of Jack, and her plans for the future, to have it spoiled by Sara.

She heard Jack's car purr to a halt, and stood up. 'I'll phone for a taxi, then go and change,' she said. She wanted to be alone for a while anyway.

She left them talking on the terrace and got into the taxi which waited patiently by Jack's Rolls-Royce. She asked the driver to drop her by the harbour, and pick her up two hours later. That would be time enough for Monique and Jack to make their plans.

Sara wandered round the shops, and felt better for being alone. It was easier, in that throng, not to think, just to relax, and stroll, and window-gaze, and she wandered round the back streets and bought an ice cream and strolled along licking it, observing the people, fascinated by them, and saw Morgan's car without surprise as it drew up several hundred yards away and stopped outside a block of ultra-modern apartments. She began to walk more quickly, saw him get out, and was about to call out to him when she saw him go round to open the passenger door. A woman got out, a tall redheaded woman dressed in a long bold print cotton skirt and white blouse. She handed something to him, bent to get something out of the Mercedes, and he locked the door. They they walked into the entrance to the apartments. The woman was laughing at something Morgan said. If he had looked round he would have seen Sara, but he didn't. He was looking at the woman.

She went back in the taxi, and her head ached with the effort it cost her not to cry. There was no sign of Monique or Jack, but she had left a note. It was very brief. 'Back soon, Love M,' it said. Sara went into her bedroom, newly tidied and cleaned, and lay on her bed. There was a perfectly reasonable explanation, of course. There must be. The woman was a business colleague, someone who worked for him. Dry-eyed, she stared at the ceiling. She had no claim on him; she knew that. She had know it all along, and if she hadn't it had been made very obvious this week. He regretted his behaviour and was making sure it never happened again. Theirs was a business relationship, an engagement in name only—no more. He had said that, once, a lifetime ago, and then yielded to temptation—she turned her head on the pillow, a lump in her throat from the effort it took to keep from weeping. She loved Morgan, but he didn't love her. Was he making love to the woman now? Sara sat up, unable to bear it any longer, and went outside by the pool. She wished Monique would return—she wished, she wished—she didn't know what she wished, only that she had never met him.

From various parts of the house came the sounds of activity, the whirr of vacuum cleaners, a snatch of song, women's voices. Sara turned and went back in to the library, found a book, and took it outside to read.

It was Morgan who came back first, three or four hours later. He looked tired. Sara had had time to work things out in her mind. She greeted him casually. 'Hello. Want a drink?'

He sat down on the terrace chair and peered at the cover of her book. 'Hmm, Simenon. Any good?'

'Yes.' She wasn't aware whether it was good or not, because she might as well have been reading a book in Arabic, but she wasn't going to tell him that.

'I'd love a coffee. Where's Monique?'

'Out with Jack. I'll get you one.' She stood up. 'Been busy?'

'Yes, fixing the catering arrangements. There'll be a van-load of stuff coming from the hotel tomorrow afternoon.'

'Good.' She walked away. What had she expected? That he would tell her where he had really been for the past three hours?

She made two cups and carried them back to the terrace. Morgan looked tired. He also looked faintly pleased about something. Sara wished that she didn't love him. She didn't want to love him. 'It's very kind of you to give me this party,' she said. She wanted to scream at him, and hit him, but she didn't. She was learning something at last, if only how to cope with the searing pain of jealousy.

'It seems a perfect idea. Celebrate your birthday and let it be known officially that we're engaged.'

'Yes it does, doesn't it?' He looked at her, puzzled, she could tell.

She sipped her coffee and gazed out towards the sea. She wished she could hurt him, but he couldn't be hurt. If it came to any sort of fight, she would be the loser, she had no illusions about that. She finished her coffee and stood up. 'Excuse me,' she said. 'I'm going for a shower.' She went into her room, locked door and window, and sat reading the book. She was going to stay there until Monique returned.

She had thought that she couldn't be hurt any more, after

that. She had adjusted to the situation. Morgan had a woman, a mistress, and Sara accepted it as best she could, and decided that life was going to go on, and she was going to enjoy the party.

She stood in her room, in darkness, at eight the following evening and she knew now that she could be hurt, even worse than she had been the previous day. Only now it was too late to back out. In an hour the guests would be arriving.

She had gone into Cannes with Monique, and Jacques had taken them because Morgan had left immediately after breakfast and that had been too early, and as they drove back with Jacques to the villa, newly coiffed, a strange thing had happened. Morgan's car had been coming towards them, Jacques had tooted his horn and saluted, and Sara had seen, just for one startled split second, someone in the front seat beside Morgan. Then the person had disappeared. She had looked back out of the rear window and a head had reappeared, and it seemed that it might have been a red head. Monique looked at her and smiled. 'Did—was there anyone with Morgan?' Sara asked.

'No! He was alone, wasn't he?'

'Oh, I must need glasses.' She felt numb, numb and sick. He was returning *from* the villa with the redhaired woman. She had tried to dismiss it from her mind, but now, in the time she was alone, about to get ready for the biggest night of her life, the sick sensation rushed back. She hadn't imagined it. Morgan had been with someone, and that someone had ducked so that Sara wouldn't see her—and it *was* the woman. He had known how long they would be at the hairdressers; he had asked Monique that morning at breakfast. He had timed it accordingly—but not well enough. Not quite well enough. Martine must have seen them. How could he? How *could* he?

Sara went to the window and looked out at the flood-lit pool. Lights blazed down from the wall above her

window, and the glow of them filled her bedroom. It was
like looking from the theatre on to a lighted stage. Later,
people would swim, if they wished—and were drunk
enough, Monique had told her.

It was time to get ready. Time to put on the best act
of her life. To pretend to be a happy bride-to-be.

The villa was a blaze of light and noise—and people. Guests
were everywhere, sitting, standing on the terrace, by the
pool, in the dining room, the hall, the library. Some had
even overflowed to the front entrance and were dancing
by the cars, and someone had left their car headlights on
so that dancers were caught in the beams, casting grotesque
shadows. The music came from speakers all around the
building, and someone, a disc jockey hired for the evening,
played a constant stream of the latest records, not too loud,
but loud enough.

It looked as though nearly all the staff from the hotel
were there, managing the buffet set out on long trestle
tables in the dining room, covered in white damask cloths,
a veritable feast. A bar had been set up in the wide hall,
and the supply of drinks was apparently never-ending. Sara
wandered round with Morgan, being introduced to everyone, being weighed up, assessed subtly or openly—and she
was calm and serene and it was a difficult rôle to play, but
play it she would. Monique drifted past, caught her arm,
whispered: 'Everyone is saying how beautiful you look,
Sara. Bravo!' Her own face was glowing. The face of a
woman who loves, and is loved.

Sara smiled at her. 'Thanks.' Morgan looked down at
them both.

'Excuse me a moment, will you?'

'Of course.' She watched him go, and Monique took a
glass of champagne from the tray of a passing waiter and
handed it to her. They stood by the open doors to the
terrace. From the swimming pool came the sound of

laughter and splashing, and occasional yells. The golden
people, the rich and beautiful people, milled around them, and
Sara thought—it's my birthday party, and it's cost a fortune
and I'm having a lovely time——

'Don't leave me, Monique,' she said.

Monique chuckled. 'Of course not. Everyone is enjoying
themselves——' But Sara wasn't listening. Over the heads of
dozens of people helping themselves to food from the buffet
table, she caught a glimpse of a familiar blaze of red hair.
Then the woman turned, as if aware of her regard, looked
steadily at her for a moment, and smiled.

'Why, Sara, what is it? You've gone white!' Monique took
hold of her arm.

'Who—is that redhaired woman?' Sara said faintly. Monique stood on tiptoe and looked across the room—but the
woman wasn't there any more.

'I can't see any redhead.'

'She was there,' answered Sara fiercely. 'I *saw* her.'

'But why—what is the matter?'

'She—was with Morgan yesterday. I saw them going into
some apartments. Oh, Monique don't you know who it is?
Please tell me! She's tall, youngish, brilliant red hair——' She
stopped. The expression on Monique's face would have been
comical at any other time. It was a mixture of dismay and
embarrassment, and she couldn't meet Sara's eyes. Sara felt as
if she was going to faint. She *knew*. She *knew*——Sara felt as if
her one last friend had betrayed her. It was like a conspiracy.
She turned to walk away, too unhappy to speak, and Monique
caught her arm.

'Wait,' she said. Sara looked at her, pulled her arm free,
and turned away. She walked in the direction the woman had
gone, but she was nowhere to be seen. Morgan was, though.
He was about to go up the stairs. He didn't see Sara. She stood
there, clutching her glass, and a woman drifted past, very
close, and whispered:

'A very jolly party, my dear. Quite the best——'

'Thank you.' Sara smiled at her, the woman smiled back tipsily and weaved a way towards a tray-laden waiter. Sara put her glass down on a table, and went towards the stairs. A couple sat on the bottom step, whispering to each other, giggling. She passed them and ran up to the wide landing that stretched the length of the upper floor. All the bedroom doors were open except Monique's—and the one next to it. Heart hammering rapidly, Sara walked towards it.

From inside the room came a woman's laughter, soft and low, and then Morgan's voice, saying something very quietly. Sara, trembling, bent to the keyhole, and the key was in it, on the other side. She reeled across the hallway, hand to mouth, stifling a sob. Dear God, he had brought her *here* as a guest, and was making love to her *here*—at her own party! She stood there for a moment quite incapable of moving away, and heard the creak of bed springs, and a laugh.

Her heart thudded in such a way that she thought she was going to die. This, this was the cruellest thing he could ever have done to her. Then he would come down, laughing, joking, and join the party, and pretend to be the loving fiancé to her again. Of course he would, and he would be laughing inwardly, and so would the woman, who would look at Sara and pity her for the fool she was.

She had to get away. To leave now.

She walked quietly, steadily down the stairs, passed the couple who, arms locked round each other, were totally oblivious to anyone, and, taking a deep breath, smiling, made her way through the guests, towards her room.

The light flooded in from the pool, and at least a dozen people were outside, laughing and talking loudly, watching a couple swimming with all their clothes on, cheering them on. They couldn't see inside the darkened bedroom, and they had their backs to it anyway because what was going on in the pool was much more fun. Sara went over

to her wardrobe, found her old suitcase, and began to fling
clothes into it. She grabbed at random, underwear, trousers,
tops, and stuffed them in. She would find a hotel for the night,
and tomorrow see about a plane home. It wouldn't be easy
slipping out unobserved, but she would manage somehow.
There was a telephone in Morgan's bedroom. She was going to
phone for a taxi to meet her at the gate.

She took off her ring and laid it on the bedside table, then
the door opened. Morgan stood there. He looked at her, then
at the open suitcase on the bed. 'What the hell are you doing?'
he demanded.

'Leaving,' she answered crisply. The feeling of nausea had
passed. She was icily cold and calm, and under control. This,
after all, wasn't the first time she had left a house in anger. She
hoped it would be the last. He closed the door, turned the key.
'No, you're not,' he said.

'I saw you with her,' she said, turning to face him. The
room was dark, but the light coming in was sufficient for her
to see the shadowy outline of him, his face a grey blur.
'Yesterday, taking her into those apartments, today, coming
back from here—and just now, I heard you upstairs. That was
the last straw, to bring your mistress *here*!'

He walked forward, grabbed hold of her, held her tightly,
and he was shaking with laughter. 'Sara,' he said, 'oh, Sara,
don't tell me you're jealous?'

'Jealous?' she shrieked. 'Of course I'm not jealous!
You're loathsome—detestable—you're bloody well welcome
to her!' and she kicked out violently at his leg, and, as he
winced and loosened his hold fractionally, she lashed out out
wildly at his face. The icy calm had gone for good. Incensed,
she twisted away as he reached for her and picked up her
brush from the dressing table, flung it at him, and followed it
with a bottle of perfume which bounced off his chest and fell
to the carpet.

He lunged forward and grabbed her, pinned her to him
so tightly that she was helpless, picked her up under one

arm, kicking and screaming, and carried her to the door.

'Right,' he said, tight-voiced. '*Right*. That does it.'

He carried her into the corridor, holding her in both arms now, and he went past his bedroom, opened a door and took her, still writhing, trying to bite his hand, up the narrow back staircase. Sara had stopped shouting. There was something so grim and determined about him that she actually felt frightened. Where was he going?

She knew a minute later when they reached the upper corridor from the opposite end. The sounds of revelry wafting from downstairs would have drowned her shouts anyway.

Morgan opened the door of the bedroom from where she had heard the telltale noises coming, went in, put her down, slammed the door shut, and locked it. The room was in darkness, the only light a faint one from the window. She heard him take the key out of the door.

'Right,' he said, as she stood trembling before him, unsure, bewildered, 'I've got the key. Do you want to fight me for it?' He put it in his trouser pocket and took his jacket off, and flung it on a chair. She could see only dim outlines of furniture. She was frightened of him. He wasn't laughing any more, he was deadly serious.

'I want to go,' she said, keeping her voice steady with difficulty.

'You're not going anywhere, Sara. We're going to talk, you and I.'

'What about? Your mistress? You make me sick!'

'She's not my mistress.'

'I heard you making love to her here, in this room.' She walked forward, towards him. 'I don't want to stay in here any longer.'

'Then try and take the key off me,' he said softly. 'Go on. I'd enjoy a fight with you.'

Sara stopped dead. 'What?'

'You heard me.' He put his hand under her chin. 'You have got me madder than any woman has any right——'

'I've got *you* mad! My God, you really do take the biscuit! You come straight from one woman's arms and——'

'I'm going to switch the light on. Tell me what you see,' he said, and there was a click. Light flooded the room. Sara blinked and looked around. The bed, neatly made up, untouched, stood in a corner against the far wall. It had been moved from its place in the middle of the wall. An easel stood in the space near the window, by it a table with tubes of oil paints neatly lined up, and brushes, and charcoal sticks. A blank canvas was pinned to the easel, and a paint-spattered overall lay on a chair beside it.

'Well?" he said softly.

'I—I don't understand,' she muttered.

'I can see that. Let me explain. My redheaded "mistress" is a painter—a portrait painter, one of the best. Her name is Estelle Fabrais. I was with her yesterday to make some arrangements. I brought her here today, while you were safely out of the way with Monique, to bring her painting materials. I came up with her to this room tonight to set it up with her, and she wanted the bed moved, to give her more space to work in. And the reason for all this is because I've commissioned her to paint your portrait as my birthday gift to you.'

Sara went slowly over to the bed and sat down on it. He came over to her and sat beside her. 'Well?' he said.

'Oh, Morgan.' She looked down at her clasped hands.

'Oh, Morgan,' he repeated. 'Is that all? I asked you a question before, I'll ask it again. Are you jealous?'

'Yes,' she whispered, 'I was.' She raised anguished eyes to him.

'Why?'

She shook her head. 'It doesn't matter——'

'Oh, yes, it does.' He put his arm round her. 'It matter very much. You have to love someone to be jealous of them

He tilted her chin to face him. He wasn't angry any more. He looked now as he had that fateful night they had spent together. 'Do you love me, Sara?'

'Yes.' It was a mere whisper.

'And I love you. Very much.' His face was tender. 'My dearest girl, don't you know why I've been so damned aloof all week? Didn't you realise why?'

'No.'

'It was because—after that wonderful night, I knew I loved you as I had never loved anyone before. But to hold you, to make love to you, as I desperately wanted—and want—to do, wasn't part of our bargain. So I—resisted.' He laughed softly. 'But—I need you, Sara. Not just as my offical fiancée, social secretary, whatever—I need *you*, and I want you very much. Will you stay here, and be my wife?'

She flung her arms round him and held him tightly. 'Yes. Yes!'

When, at last, they rejoined the party, hardly surprised to find they hadn't been missed at all, it was to announce the date of their wedding.

A WORD ABOUT THE AUTHOR

While many Harlequin authors say that writing has always been in their blood, Mary Wibberley claims that as a child the idea of being a writer never even entered her head. For her, the future always meant becoming an artist, or perhaps a Wimbledon tennis champion!

But after marriage and the birth of her daughter, Mary thought she'd give writing a try. So she crept downstairs one night and began covering pages of paper with notes.

Her first novel did not meet with success, nor did her second, third, fourth, fifth, sixth or seventh. But to her surprise and delight, her eighth attempt, *The Black Niall* (Romance #1717), was accepted and published in 1973.

Mary Wibberley likes her heroines—and her heroes—to have a sense of humor. And no matter how hard she plans her characters, she finds that they take on personalities of their own. In fact, as she sits down in the morning to work, Mary will often wonder, "What on earth is going to happen today?"

4 FREE
Harlequin Romances